Jacob's

Exile

Book three of:

Jacob's Struggle

By: Boris Copper

DEDICATION

This book is dedicated to Jacob Stall, the young boy who inspired it,
and to the fine members of *Notebored*, the online group who
gave the author so many valuable crits and encouragement.
Without them all, this story would never have been conceived let alone birthed.

ISBN: 0615956998
ISBN-13: 978-0615956992

CONTENTS

Acknowledgments   i

1   Exiled   1

2   Captured   6

3   The Spring Festival   9

4   The Party's Over   13

5   Dawn of a New Life   18

6   Jacob Can Shoot!   25

7   Be Someone's One?   29

8   Fight for Meleitha   35

9   A Bear Forever?   42

10   Musket Repair   48

11   Injin Smith   52

12   Exiled Again   56

13   Terms of Exile   62

14   Rogue Injin   67

15   Mano e Mana   71

16   Fort Detroit   79

17   Shoshanna   83

18   Take Me Home   89

19   New York   95

20   Can I Come Home?   97

21   The Bounty Hunters   101

22   Behind Bars   104

23   Let's Make a Deal   108

24   Welcome Home, Son   111

25   Hannah   117

26   The Weddings   120

27   I am Iroquois   124

28   Zacharia   126

29   Free At Last   130

30   Now It's My War   133

31   Ya Wanna Fight?   137

32   Mr. O'Malley's Advice   142

33   Kaskaskia   145

34   Mateo's Burden   149

35   Injin War Dance   152

36   Camp Hunger   156

37   Attack on Vencennes   159

38   Dan'l Morgan   163

39   A Bit o' Smithin'   166

40   Jacob Quits   170

41   Cat and Mouse   173

42   The Cowpen   177

43   Villains Rewarded   185

44   Jacob's Children   191

1   Exile

April, 1771

Jacob lay shivering in the dark abandoned cabin.

How long have I been running?

It had been weeks certainly, maybe months since the horrible day when the men had come from Wynnewood to arrest him for the murder of his old master. The time since had been one long miserable blur of narrow escapes. At least he had been spared an adventure the past few days.

Maybe I've finally lost 'em.

He refused to believe it; he had been disappointed before. He shifted his weight trying to find a comfortable position. The day he had spent huddled in a pine tree watching for pursuers had been miserable, but he believed he preferred it to the horrid darkness spent lying on a hard dirt floor.

At least I'm out of the wind.

The cabin was ideal, for it had a hole in the rear wall, and was built into a stand of pines which would conceal his escape if he had to use it. He would not have dared spend the night in the cabin if it had not. He knew he should be thankful he had found the cabin. But he did wish he dared to light a fire; he was so cold.

He could not help wishing he were sleeping warm and safe beside his brother and rejoicing in his betrothal to Hannah.

Why, oh why, did those men have to discover my whereabouts the very day her father was to give her to me?

1

He had not killed the old brute; Mateo, his brother, had, but no one knew that but the two brothers and Jacob had made Mateo swear he would never reveal it. Jacob would far rather die than see his brother die. Besides, Mateo had only killed their master to prevent him killing Jacob. But since both Jacob and Mateo had been indentured, they had known they would have to flee. For so many wonderful years they had evaded detection; they had thought themselves safe.

He wondered how long it would be before it would be safe for him to return to his brother and Hannah. He knew it could be a very long time.

When he had been first forced to flee, he had assumed he would simply have to evade the men Miranda, his old master's daughter, had sent from Wynnewood.

He chuckled to remember how easily he had lost them.

But he had very soon discovered she had, in addition to sending those men, caused fliers to be sent everywhere with a reward on his head . . . a large reward. He had never realized before how much power money wielded. It seemed everyone in the entire colony was on his trail seeking that reward.

I don't even know where I am anymore; it's been days since I've seen a settlement.

He struggled not to despair, and felt self pity rise to engulf him.

Why must I be separated from all I love . . . again? Why did God allow this to happen to me?

But he remembered the words of Job: 'Shall I accept blessings from the Lord but not adversity?'

And he felt the small book of Psalms which he had found tucked with the food Mrs. O'Malley had provided for his escape. When he had first found it, he had been tempted to toss it aside; of what use was a book of Psalms in his dilemma? It only took up valuable space and added weight. But he had kept it and read from it when he could. It had been more comfort than he could have dreamed. More than once he had blessed Mrs. O'Malley for her foresight and generosity in giving it to him.

He wished he had light enough to read from it now.

David the King was pursued as I am, with even less justification, yet in the end God delivered him. I must trust he shall deliver me.

He remembered his grandfather saying, "You never know what God has planned for your future; the important thing is to survive." He grinned wryly. *What if you have naught but misery in your future?*

But he remembered asking that question of himself on the long cold nights in his master's barn when he had felt like giving up the struggle. Then he could not have imagined a brother like Mateo or friends like Mr. Wallace, Mr. O'Malley, or the Gerbers, much less a gal like Hannah. How much he would have missed had he not survived and persevered. His old grandfather had been right after all.

He froze, his contemplations interrupted. He knew not what was amiss, but his senses had detected danger. He rolled out of his blanket, took up his rifle, and crawled to the chink low in the front wall. That was another fortuitous aspect of the cabin he had noticed; it enabled him to see outside without revealing himself.

He saw two, no, three, men creeping toward the cabin. Who were they? Were they pursuers or strangers who meant him no harm? The fact that they seemed to be stalking toward the cabin was an ominous sign, but he needed to know with what type of men he was dealing.

One was briefly revealed by the faint moonlight. His head was bald except for a ridge of hair running across his scalp from front to back. They were Iroquois!

All of the lurid bloody tales he had been told of the Iroquois rose up before Jacob and he scurried as fast as he could to his escape hole, and squeezed through. He had left his blanket and other provisions behind, but it could not be helped. Only escape mattered now.

He slipped as quickly yet noiselessly through the pines as he could knowing it would be but moments before the fiends would be on his trail, and then he ran trying to remember all of the tricks for throwing pursuers off one's trail.

God in heaven, have I not enough men seeking my blood? Why must these vipers seek it as well? Please help me escape.

He did not wish to die.

At least white men would have killed me quickly and mercifully had they captured me. Have I gone through all my troubles and misery to elude them only to face a horrid tortuous death at the hand of these fiends?

He ran harder.

* * * *

Jacob glanced at the sun. It had risen, crawled excruciatingly across the sky, and was finally low on the horizon. Still his pursuers followed, and still Jacob fled. Yet he began to allow himself to hope.

If I can remain free until dark, I may yet escape them.

But he was so weary and hungry.

Shall I ever reach the crest of this hill?

It seemed he had been climbing forever but he had had no choice for the Iroquois were both to his left and right as well as behind. It took all he had just to keep ahead of them.

Finally the ground leveled off, and he increased his speed; if he could just put a little distance between himself and the fiends pursuing him . . .

He burst from the trees, and skidded to a stop in horror. Before him was a vast void.

He looked over the cliff at the ground far below, at least a hundred feet he guessed. He saw no path down. He nearly collapsed in despair. It was over. It was only a matter of minutes before the Iroquois would be upon him; he had no escape.

Then he noticed a great oak tree growing at the base of the cliff; its upper branches were a mere twenty feet or so below the cliff edge. Throwing caution aside, Jacob ran and leaped.

For horrifying seconds he fell, and then crashed into the green canopy of the oak. Limbs snapped and broke as they clawed, scrapped, and pummeled him. But Jacob kept his arms and legs close to his body, forced himself to remain limp, and trusted the limbs to slow his descent. He knew the best way to avoid a broken bone was to remain limber, and he did not wish to have an extremity snagged and wrenched from him.

He bounced from limb to limb like a great ball, but his speed was slowing.

He finally ventured to grab at a pliable branch. It bowed, and swung him toward the center of the tree. Too late he saw a huge branch in his path; he and it collided with a horrible blow, but he grabbed hold and clung to it. His ribs screamed, and he could not breathe, but he was finally stopped. Trying not to moan, he struggled atop the branch, and lay.

After a moment he surveyed his aching body. He found that although he had received a good many bruises, he had broken no bones. Ignoring his body's objections, he moved further into the tree's foliage, and concealed himself from the cliff top.

He waited.

Is it more dangerous to move while there may be someone on the cliff to observe me, or to remain here while they find a path down the cliff?

He did not know.

He saw that the branches of the tree intertwined with those of a tree to its left and he worked his way to them, leaped into the next tree and then into a third. That had been one of Mateo's favorite tricks, and a successful one. The sun had lowered enough that the base of the cliff was in shadow; he needed to find a way out of the tiny valley he was in while he could still see, or find a place to hide.

His eye fell upon a great fallen tree. He could see midway along it a large hollow filled with leaves and other vegetative debris. He resolved to attempt to gain that hollow and conceal himself therein. With little difficulty he did so. He congratulated himself that he had left no trail from the oak into which he had cast himself to the log.

He worked himself and his rifle into the debris trying hard to leave no trace. The dead leaves and other vegetation were damp and very odorous, but he found their decay was generating a very pleasant heat. For the first time in weeks, he was warm.

And he was soon asleep.

2   Captured

April, 1771

Jacob awoke when his rifle was snatched from his grasp and he looked up to find the horribly painted face of an Iroquois warrior grinning down upon him. He had no choice but surrender.

He squirmed from his hollow, followed his captor from the tree to where his fellows awaited them, and had his hands bound securely. After the warmth of the hollow, his damp clothes exposed to the raw wind were frigid and chaffing. But they soon dried and warmed as he was forced to trot very fast along a trail he could hardly discern.

Where are they taking me and why have they captured me? He tried asking them both in English and Algonquin, but received no reply. He remembered Woosamequin telling him the Iroquois language was completely different from that of other Indians. It seemed he could neither understand them nor they him.

He learned differently that night when they made camp. One Iroquois at least could communicate in Algonquin for he ordered Jacob to build a fire. To Jacob's surprise, he was well fed and assigned a place quite near the fire. He was bound, but not uncomfortably so and, due to his long fast walk and generous meal, was soon asleep.

The following day was much like the first, but late that afternoon, a scout returned and made a report to the others. Jacob soon found himself securely bound to a tree, the warriors prepared themselves for battle, and left him. Clearly they did not fear his escape.

Indeed, despite his best efforts, he was unable to free himself.

Eventually three of the warriors returned, Jacob was cut loose, ordered to carry the supplies they had left behind, and led swiftly through the forest. Soon they emerged into what clearly had been a hunting camp; there were a multitude of skins and mounds of dried meat.

With a nauseating shock Jacob saw that five Indians lay dead in grotesque positions, several with their brains bashed in, all of them scalped. Two Indians yet living were bound to trees at the periphery of the clearing.

But Jacob was given no time to adapt to this new reality for he was ordered to build a fire and the Iroquois and he ate. It felt surreal and somewhat sacrilegious to calmly eat in the midst of such carnage, but Jacob had no idea how long it might be before he was again fed. So he did his best to ignore his surroundings and ate. When the meal was over, he was bound to a tree, and the warriors addressed themselves to the Indian captives.

They went to the first of them, and Jacob was appalled to watch as one warrior took out a knife. Yet, as he watched the poor Indian writhe as the warrior sliced his arm, Jacob found it did not evoke the terror or horror it should; he felt numb inside. It was as if he was watching the torture from a vast distance of time and space. His mind could not grasp one man treating another in such a manner, and as such, it did not seem real.

A howl of agony reverberated through the forest and sent tremors up Jacob's spine as a sizable piece of skin was ripped free from the poor victim. The Indian pled for mercy. With a scowl, one of the warriors pulled out his war club and bashed the man's brains in. His scalp was taken, and his body cast sprawling from the camp. The Iroquois turned to their second captive.

But that Indian stood stoically, and stared into the eyes of his tormentors despite their torture. He was soon a bloody abomination. Still the torture continued, and still Jacob felt nothing.

Shall this be my fate? he thought calmly. Even that failed to evoke an emotion. *If it is, which example shall I follow?* Clearly a plea for mercy would result in a quick death, but it would be a dishonorable death. *Yet is the agony of the second worth bearing?*

He did not know, but he resolved he would not give his captors the satisfaction of seeing him beg if he could help it.

To his astonishment the Iroquois suddenly desisted from their brutality, spoke in a friendly mien to the miserable wretch commending him for his fortitude, and offered him food and water. It was not long however before the poor Indian succumbed to loss of blood, fainted, and finally died. The Iroquois respectfully unbound him, and laid him out beside the bodies of his comrades. Then they came for Jacob.

But they merely moved him to a place beside the fire and settled down to sleep as if nothing extraordinary had transpired.

Jacob lay for some time wondering why he had been able to witness such things and yet feel nothing. *What kind of a fiend am I that such things could leave me unmoved?* He despised himself. *How can I not care?* But he did not care. He found himself able to consider even his own fate as if it did not concern him. *Why did they torture and kill the Indians but not me? Why am I still alive?*

He began to drift off to sleep, but then the numbness and uncaring fled, and were replaced by revulsion, pity, and cold terror. Over and over he retched until he had nothing left to spew. Then he lay trembling and sweating. Desperately he struggled against his bonds until his wrists and ankles were raw and bleeding.

But it was a useless battle.

In the end he surrendered to his fate and spent the remainder of the night wishing God had allowed him to die before he had witnessed such evil.

3   The Spring Festival

April, 1771

On the evening of the third day, his captors led Jacob
through the gate of a stockade inside which were about a dozen
long bark buildings radiating out from a central courtyard.

Jacob stared fascinated at these buildings which had no
sides or roof, but rather rose from the ground and arched so that
they appeared to be enormous logs half buried in the ground.
They were twenty feet in diameter and sixty feet long and had no
chimneys, but smoke rose from holes at the apex of the arch.

The ground between the buildings contained many small
garden plots well tilled and ready to be planted. Jacob was
impressed. These people were clearly hard working, skilled, and
orderly. He looked from his captors to the village. It was difficult
to reconcile the horrendous savagery of the one with the tranquil
order of the other. Yet this was clearly their village, the men were
being welcomed as fathers and brothers. The men of the village
each wore a skull cap made of woven white feathers with one hawk
feather standing up at an angle toward the rear. The caps made
the men look peaceful and intellectual.

The mien of the welcome was also incongruous. These
bloodthirsty cruel fiends were greeting, and being greeted by, the
women and children with doting affection; it was difficult to

believe these very men had only a day earlier been dashing the brains from foes.

But Jacob was jerked from his ruminations by one of his captors returning to lead him into a small fenced enclosure. There his bonds were severed, and he was given water and a generous supply of surprisingly good food. The children and women gathered around the prison freely discussed him, but no one presumed to abuse him. This was not at all the treatment Jacob had expected.

The Iroquois brave who spoke Algonquin came and, leaning upon the fence, spoke quite friendly with Jacob. Jacob saw he also now wore a skull cap.

"We were fortunate," the brave said, "We arrived just in time for the spring festival. Have you ever seen a spring festival?"

"No," Jacob replied. "This is my first visit to the Iroquois." It was difficult to keep the sarcasm from his voice. Still, the man was being friendly; Jacob preferred to try to keep him that way. Yet he wondered why he was.

"Then I expect you'll find this interesting. When I was young I could hardly wait for the spring festival. It is the high point of the year." To Jacob's astonishment, the brave actually grinned at him. "Seven days of feasting."

Jacob struggled to conceal his astonishment. Could this be the same man who had driven him for days with harsh curses and frightful threats? He was now telling him of his childhood anticipation of a feast?

"Ah," cried the brave with a laugh, "here come the dogs." He reached an arm through the posts, and elbowed Jacob. "You'll enjoy this."

Jacob looked to where he was pointing, and saw two old women each lead a pure white dog on a leash into the center of the yard. All the children of the village lined up around the yard's periphery. Even Jacob could feel their excited anticipation.

When the children were ready, the women released their dogs, and the children swarmed in upon them, but the dogs were too fast for them. Bounding between the children, they escaped between two of the longhouses with the children in fast pursuit.

In and out of the yard, across the readied garden plots, sometimes in and out of a longhouse if a dog spied an open door, the chase wended. Occasionally a dog would be captured by a fortunate child. Other children would immediately leap upon him, but he would somehow squirm free. Finally one of the dogs did not break free; a veritable mound of boys and girls subdued it. This unfortunate dog was led to one of two posts which were planted in the center of the yard, and there tied. Then the adults helped the children capture the remaining dog which was tied to the second post.

Jacob was surprised to discover he had indeed enjoyed watching the chase, but now that it was over and the dogs were captured, he remembered he was himself a captive. The dread of a horrible unknown fate returned. He reminded himself these happy laughing people were the savage fiends he had been warned about, and he was in their power.

His fear was not allayed for everyone returned to the periphery of the yard, even the children stood silent, and an aura of doom permeated the village.

An old shaman entered the yard carrying a war club. Standing between the two dogs, he chanted a long melodious prayer and then, starting with the first dog caught, bashed each of their heads in. Drawing a knife from his belt, he quickly and efficiently disemboweled them. Taking a heart in each hand, he lifted them to the sky and faced each of the four points of the compass. Then he dropped prostrate upon the ground, and began a low moaning chant.

Instantly a file of young warriors, painted hideously for war, poured from a longhouse and began to dance around the shaman, and two women came, each bearing a pan which she set at the head of a dog. The shaman dipped a brush into one pan, and began to paint the first dog red. The dancing warriors began to howl, and another file of dancers poured from another house, this one composed of young women, naked but for ribbons and a few feathers. They wove in and out between the men until they had circled the yard, and then both groups formed a long line which danced into and out of each longhouse of the village.

Meanwhile, having finished painting the second dog yellow, the shaman hung each upon one of the poles and then began to chant another long monotonous prayer. Having completed their circuit, the two groups of dancers disappeared within their respective houses, and at last the chant fell silent.

Scarcely had it done so than the village erupted with noise and activity. From every longhouse emerged women bearing platters of food, and suddenly bottles of whiskey seemed to be in every man's hand and were freely passed about, even to the women and children. Clearly the feast had begun.

It went long into the night.

If I but wait, they'll all be drunk and sleeping. Jacob remembered there was a small corral just outside the gate of the stockade. He had seen half a dozen horses there. *If the braves guarding the horses are allowed to drink also, I should be able to scale this fence and steal a horse. By morning I could be miles away, and my pursuers shall be hung over.*

But alas, although many of the Iroquois did indeed drink themselves into a stupor, many did not. He would not be escaping that night.

He wished the talkative brave would return. He longed to ask him the meaning of the ritual. If he was to have no chance to escape, he would like to learn what he could. Besides, he was lonely.

But if this was the fate of the dogs, what shall be my fate?

4   The Party's Over

May, 1771

Six days of feasting had slowly passed; the seventh was nearly over.

Jacob faced the end of the feast with both terror and relief. Terror because, while he had concluded the Iroquois intended him no evil while the feast continued, who knew what they might do when it was ended? But relief because living in the fearful anticipation of what they intended had been almost more misery than he could abide.

Come what may, my wait shall soon be over.

He had spent the week of the feast in his small cage watching the dogs slowly fill with maggots and decay. He had wished his cage was further from their posts, especially when the wind was from their direction. He had also wished he had been allowed from his cage to relieve himself; the pile of his excrement was becoming offensive.

But beyond those conditions, he had had nothing about which to complain; he had been very well fed and, although the nights had often been cold, the Iroquois had supplied him with a bear skin which had proven very warm and waterproof.

Indeed, he had been treated with a surprising deference. He had often wondered why he was. In his darker moments he had worried he was being fattened for a final feast at the end of the week; many Indians had darkly hinted the Iroquois practiced cannibalism, but he had shoved those worries aside.

However, as the week had proceeded he had learned to recognize many of the villagers, and had noticed one older woman who had come every day and watched him keenly. She had been often accompanied by two women who Jacob guessed were about his own age. The three would walk about him, observe him, and then gather to discuss him, often at some length.

The other villagers had also watched him, but none so regularly nor as acutely as had these three.

Shall these three women be the ones who shall be responsible for roasting me?

He considered asking the Algonquin speaking brave about them, but was afraid to do so although the brave, who Jacob had learned was named Shikellamy, had become very friendly. He was not sure he wanted to learn his fate.

As the sun sank toward the horizon, a fire was built before the two posts upon which the dogs hung, and a large cauldron half filled with water was placed in its center. Jacob did not like the sight of that; the rumors of cannibalism were beginning to seem only too true.

But, as he watched, the two dogs were removed from the posts and laid in the fire, one on each side of the cauldron. The smell of their scorched hair did not improve their odor. After a time one dog, Jacob noticed it had been the second one killed, was removed from the fire, and dropped into the kettle.

The other was allowed to burn to ashes while the kettle steamed. Then the fire was doused, the ashes of the burned dog were carefully gathered, and a bit was strewn upon the door of each longhouse. The remaining ashes of the dog were placed in a shallow bowl, and the villagers formed a long line by families, and soberly filed past as the shaman rubbed a streak upon their foreheads.

Then the shaman and an assistant reached into the cauldron with long forks, removed the boiled carcass of the second dog, and laid it upon a plank. Again the line filed past; this time each villager tore a bit of flesh from the dog, and consumed it. Jacob had to struggle not to vomit.

When they were finished, Jacob was alarmed to find he became the center of attention.

This is it at last. God of Heaven have mercy upon my soul. Grant me strength to endure whatever is coming.

Everyone had gathered in a circle about his prison, and the chief of the village came to stand before it, accompanied by the older woman who had paid such attention to him. They were joined by the two younger women, and three young children, a boy and two girls.

The chief and the older woman stood and discussed him at some length, and then the chief came forward, and addressed Jacob in Algonquin.

"Taghahjute has accepted you to replace her son who died last fall. She needs a man to be a brother to her daughters, a father to her grandchildren, and a provider for them all."

Jacob regarded the group gathered before him. So these were the woman's daughters and grandchildren and she was proposing to adopt him, expecting him to provide for them all?

"Will you be her son?"

Jacob wondered what would happen if he refused. He also wondered how he could provide for so many without his weapons.

"How can I provide for so many without a gun?"

The chief lifted his chin and considered him. "Your weapons shall be given Taghahjute. When she wishes you to hunt, she shall give them to you and have some other men accompany you until she is confident she can trust you. Earn her trust, and you shall be free to retain them. You shall then be as any other man among us."

Jacob did not believe he had any choice but to accept their terms, so he said, "I will be her son."

The chief immediately stepped forward, and opened the gate. Flanked by the chief and his new mother and followed by her family, he was led to the cauldron. There the shaman dipped a finger into the ashes and streaked it across Jacob's forehead. Then he indicated the dog carcass.

Jacob's stomach revolted, but he knew what he was expected to do. He held his breath, ripped off a minute bit of flesh, and swallowed it whole. The chief beside him said, "Your name is now Techusin."

Suddenly the village was filled with noise, smiles, and laughter. Jacob was surrounded, welcomed, and made to sit beside his new mother, sisters, and children while platters of food appeared and were placed before them.

Shikellamy, the Algonquin speaker, came to translate for him. When the festivities ebbed and Jacob had time, he dared to ask him the meaning of the ritual regarding the dogs. He learned the ritual was done each spring; upon the first dog captured was placed all of the wrongs the villagers had done in the past year. When it was burned, the Iroquois believed their wrongs were consumed and carried to the sky where Teharonhiawagon, the Master of Life, dispersed them to the four winds. When the villagers consumed the second dog, they were made one people just as the dog had been one dog. When the smear of ash had been placed upon Jacob's forehead, all of his sins had been dispersed also, and when he had consumed the dog he had become an Iroquois, a Seneca, and a member of their village as well as a member of his mother's family.

Jacob remembered one of God's ordinances for the Jews was very similar. In that case it had been two goats instead of dogs and the scapegoat had not been killed, only driven into the wilderness. But the principle, he realized, was very similar.

Much later he was led to his new family's longhouse which he found was shared with two other families. To Jacob's joy, he found his mother, Taghahjute, did indeed have his rifle, his North Carolina tomahawk, and his knife which she gave to one of the men of the other families to guard. Jacob did not care about the knife, despite having been given him by Mr. O'Malley, there was nothing special about it, but he did rejoice to see he would regain his rifle and tomahawk.

His mother directed him to a platform built along the wall; there lay a pack which, when unrolled, contained all he had left in the cabin when he had fled including, he was happy to see, his small book of Psalms. The Iroquois had withheld nothing from him.

One of his new sisters handed him a mat and, following their example, he spread it upon the floor, and lay upon it. One by one, everyone fell asleep.

There is no one still awake to guard me, Jacob marveled. *I could simply get up and leave.* But he did not expect he would get very far and was sure he would not receive gentle treatment when again captured. *Besides, where can I go?* The only place he wished to go was Berks County and there he knew he could not go even if he escaped the Iroquois.

Remaining with the Iroquois seemed as good an option as any he had; they did not seem to intend him harm. His new mother and sisters had treated him with deference and respect, and the three children had watched him with large, curious, but friendly eyes. He rather liked them.

He rolled over and allowed himself to drift off to sleep.

5　Dawn of a New Life

May, 1771

The next morning Jacob was awakened by a nudge from the foot of Atotarho, his new 'son'.

"Satgeh," the boy said. He motioned with his hand for Jacob to get up. "Sadya'dohaeh."

Jacob saw all of the men and boys of the longhouse were leaving. He rose and followed.   Outside they were joined by the other males of the village who filed out of the walls of the stockade.

Jacob had observed this exodus of the males when he had been imprisoned in his cage; it seemed to be a ritual observed each morning. *Now I shall learn its meaning.*

Atotarho was joined by several other boys, and a lively conversation ensued between them which seemed to primarily concern Jacob. Jacob liked watching and listening to them, he liked Atotarho, but he wished he knew what they were saying.

Then again, perhaps it is just as well if I do not understand. He chuckled to himself. At least they all seemed friendly toward him.

He saw they had come to a stream, and everyone began to strip off their garments, and to bathe. Jacob was very self conscious; he had never bathed in public before, but his 'son' pointed his chin at the water, and demanded, "Sadya'dohaeh."

Jacob obeyed.

The water was very cold, but once he had overcome his shyness, he found the experience very pleasant. Many of the boys were splashing each other and laughing, even some of the men were joining in. Jacob was watching them when his side received an enormous splash.

Oh, it was cold!

He looked to where it had come, and found the impish, half afraid face of one of Atotarho's friends. "Oh ho," Jacob cried as he dropped to his knees so he was submerged to his armpits. He had learned in water fights with Mateo that it is much better to be submerged in cold water than to be splashed by it. *So you want a fight, eh?* He was glad, and swept the largest wave of water he could back at the boy.

He was immediately attacked from the rear, and soon had four lithe young bodies doing their best to force his head under the water. It was a glorious battle with Jacob flinging them from him and dunking them until he was too tired to continue and dragged himself to the shore with the boys clinging to him like leaches. He threw himself and them to the ground laughing with them.

I could get used to starting my days like this.

But then he realized Atotarho was not among his attackers; he was standing to one side and regarding him soberly. Jacob was unable to read his face, and disengaged himself from the boys, reclothed himself, and led his 'son' back to the village.

Why does he not like me? How can I show him I wish to be friends?

Hardly had they re-entered the gate of the village when he heard the cheerful call, "Techusin". He had just remembered that was his new name, when his oldest 'daughter' appeared and grabbed his hand.

What is her name again? Oh, yes. Melietha.

He grinned down upon her. "Good morning, Melietha." He could see she was pleased he had remembered her name. He saw a lock of her hair was dangling in her face and hiding her left eye. It made her look winsome, but he gently reached out and tucked it behind her ear, and then allowed her to lead him into their longhouse and to where his younger 'sister', he did not remember her name, was stirring what appeared to be some form of porridge.

She smiled at them, handed them each a bowl, and ladled a generous portion into each.

"Nya weh, Sivathahae," said the girl.

Sivathahae. Yes, that's her name . . . Does 'nya weh' mean 'thank you'? He decided to try it. "Nya weh, Sivathahae."

To his pleasure, it seemed he had guessed correctly, for she nodded, and said something in return. Unfortunately, Melietha had erupted with a torrent of words at the same time so he did not hear what Sivathahae said. *It is too bad. Now I do not know to say, 'you are welcome' or whatever its equivalent is.*

But he could not help grinning at the girl. She was so excited to hear him speak Iroquois. The stray lock of hair had escaped her ear, and was again obscuring her vision.

"Sadyeh," her aunt ordered, and she stopped talking, and sat.

Jacob followed her example.

"Sadekho:nyah."

Melietha dipped her fingers into the porridge, and licked them off, and Jacob again imitated her. It was very satisfying; he wished he could tell Sivathahae he liked it, but he did not know how, so settled for smiling and nodding. Fortunately she seemed to understand.

When the bowl was finished, he sat wondering what he should do; what would be expected of him? He considered asking for the brave who spoke Algonquin, but found he could not remember his name. But then Melietha rose and held out her hand to him.

He stood and took it, and she led him to the table where Sivathahae had used a knife to dice up some dried vegetables. Melietha pointed at the knife, and said, "A:share." She glanced at him. "A:share. Sanigohaeda's geh?"

So I am to have a language lesson.

"A:share," he repeated. He was rewarded by a smile.

"Ehe" She pointed at the table. "Atekhwa:ra"

"Ashekawa."

She burst out laughing. "Atekhwa:ra"

"Ah-tek-wah-rah"

She again laughed at him.

I like hearing her laugh. I like seeing her laugh. She is a very charming girl. I wonder how old she is. He decided she was seven or eight.

"Atekhwa:ra," she repeated.

"Atekhwa:ra."

"Ehc'!" She pointed again at the knife. "Deho'de' togyeh?"

For an awful moment Jacob could not remember, but then answered, "A:share."

"Dogehs." She pointed at the table. "Deho'de' togyeh?"

"Atekhwa:ra"

"Ehe'" She grinned up at him, and then the grin grew impish. She pointed at her little sister. "So:ne' togyeh?"

Jacob shrugged. "A girl?" How could he tell her what she was when she had not told him what the Iroquois word was?

But Melietha shook her head, and demanded, "So:ne' togyeh?"

Maybe that means, "What is her name?" "Ailantha?"

"Ehe'"

There came a knock at the door, and his 'mother' who Jacob realized had been watching them with amusement, called, "Gajih."

Shikellamy, the Algonquin speaking brave, entered. Jacob remembered his name now that he saw him. Shikellamy nodded at Jacob, and said, "Sgeno. I have come to translate for you."

Jacob was rather sorry. He had been enjoying his lesson. He looked into Melietha's eyes, nodded at her, and smiled. "Nya weh."

She grinned, and released a torrent of words.

Shikellamy listened to her, grinned, and then translated. "Um . . . she said you are welcome, she will be happy to do it again soon, she thinks you are smart, and she likes you." He had used far fewer words than she had.

Jacob grinned at the girl. "Tell her I like her too."

Shikellamy did so, and, to Jacob's alarm, Melietha leaped into his arms, he only just managed to catch her. He looked at Shikellamy, but he seemed to approve, so Jacob returned the hug the girl was giving him. He had never hugged or been hugged by a girl before; Hannah did not count, she was his intended, not a child. But he enjoyed it.

He released her, and she stood staring up at him with glee. *Now what do I do?*

To his relief, Shikellamy addressed his 'mother'. They conversed briefly, and then his mother presented Jacob with a skull cap like those worn by the other men of the village. Shikellamy told him the single feather identified him as a Seneca. But he also showed him patterns woven into the hat, patterns which further identified him as a member of: the Turtle Clan, the Tetherasingan Ohwachira, and finally, the fireside of his mother's sister.

Jacob realized the hats were as informative as the shields of the noble families of Europe.

Shikellamy then informed Jacob his mother wanted him to gather dry wood to replenish the wood pile outside the longhouse.

Jacob was happy to accept the task. He thought he would be accompanied by men to guard him, but was allowed to go into the forest with only Atotarho by his side.

What could he do to prevent my fleeing? Nothing but run back and alert the village. But how can they know I would not harm him so he couldn't alert them?

He would not harm him, of course; he would never harm a boy.

But they do not know that.

He suspected they were not as alone as they seemed.

He soon was impressed by the boy; Atotarho proved to be a very hard worker and strong for his size.

I wonder how old he is, nine probably, but he could easily be a year or even two older or younger.

He remembered wondering the same thing about Mateo when first they had met. Then too there had been a language barrier hindering them.

God in heaven, how I miss him.

He resolutely shoved his thoughts of Mateo aside and concentrated on gathering wood and transporting loads of it back to their longhouse. He could tell as the day progressed that his 'mother' was pleased.

That night he was very hungry, and looked forward to the stew his 'sister' was cooking. But then he learned it contained dog meat. Apparently dogs were consumed on a regular basis, not only ritually. Jacob was sorely tempted to put aside his scruples and eat it, for the stew smelled very enticing, but dogs were very unclean animals, nearly as unclean as swine. He reluctantly indicated he was not hungry.

He found everyone was looking at him skeptically, and his 'mother' asked, "Te' sadekho:nyah?"

He was not sure what she had asked, but shook his head.

Atotarho was sent for Shikellamy. When he had come and conversed with Jacob's 'mother', he said, "She wants to know why you refuse to eat. No one believes you are not hungry."

What can I say? How can I make them understand? He decided to try telling them the truth.

"I am a Jew." He paused. *They do not know what a Jew is. How can I explain it?* He decided not to try. "I know you do not know what a Jew is, but . . ." He stopped disconcerted. He was going to say God had commanded the Jews to not eat dog meat, but he did not know the word for 'god'. Did the Iroquois even know of God?

He looked at Shikellamy. "I do not know the name for the one who made all things."

"You mean Teharonhiawagon?"

"Did he make the Earth and all that is in it?"

"Yes."

"Teharonhiawagon, then. He commanded my people to eat only certain animals. I am forbidden to eat dogs except on occasions such as the spring feast."

23

Shikellamy translated his words to his new family. He could tell his 'mother' and 'sisters' were distressed, but they shook their heads and, after his 'mother' had spoken, Shikellamy told him this was all they had; having had no man for the past months, meat was scarce.

"Tell them I do not mind, I shall be all right until morning."

Shikellamy looked at him respectfully, and translated. His family also seemed impressed, and Shikellamy left.

Jacob's stomach rumbled; he could not help it. He wondered if he had done the right thing.

But then Melietha spoke to her mother, who nodded. Turning to Jacob, the girl flapped her arms, and quacked. Jacob grinned, and nodded. Yes he could eat a duck.

Melietha jumped up, ran out of the longhouse, and reappeared a few minutes later with a chunk of meat nearly the size of her hand. She handed it to Jacob with a smile.

"Nya weh," Jacob said; he was very glad he remembered how to thank her. *That was really very nice of her.* He looked at the meat. It was raw, but he did not want to hurt her feelings and, as hungry as he was, thought he could eat it raw.

He began to put it to his mouth, but Sivathahae snatched it away. "Sekho:nyah," she scolded. She smiled at his discomfort, speared the meat with a stick, and put it to roast over the fire.

Jacob was glad, and it was not long before it was returned to him smelling delicious. Not only had his 'sister' cooked it, she had sprinkled some form of herb upon it each time she had turned it. Jacob tried it, and found it as good as it smelled.

He looked over at Sivathahae, smiled, and inclined his head. "Nya weh."

6   Jacob can Shoot!

August, 1771

Jacob stood with Cicaho, and watched the stag feeding in the meadow. Cicaho was the leader of the hunting expedition, and an intimidating and skillful man. This was the third time Jacob had hunted with him, and each time he had been impressed by his woodcraft. He had learned a good deal from him.

Cicaho shook his head. "We must let him go." He waved his hand at the hills behind the stag. "Before any could circle him, he would disappear." He grinned at Jacob. "Too bad. We could all have feasted tonight."

Jacob nodded, and glanced back to where Shikellamy with his two sons, Cicaho's three sons, and Atotarho stood waiting in the brush. *It is indeed too bad. If only Cicaho could get beyond the stag, the eight of us could easily have herded him within his range.*

He felt proud that Cicaho had chosen him to confer with instead of Shikellamy. Although, in truth, Shikellamy was a mediocre hunter. Though skillful in slipping through the forest without a sound, it was easy to see his heart was not in it. Hunting for him was a necessary chore, not a pleasure.

But, even after several months with the Iroquois, or Hodenosaunee, as he had learned they preferred to be called, Jacob still sometimes found it hard to understand what Cicaho said. Fortunately the man was patient and skilled at pantomiming what he wanted.

He looked again at the stag grazing complacently. *He no doubt is aware of us, but he also knows the range of our muskets.* As if to prove Jacob's thought, the stag raised his head, and stared directly at him before returning to his grass. It was like a challenge, and Jacob looked down upon his rifle. The stag was beyond the range of a musket, but not beyond his rifle's.

"I believe I could reach him," he whispered to Cicaho. "May I try?"

Cicaho glanced at him, laughed silently, but shrugged. "You'll only waste your powder, but why not?"

Jacob wet his far sight, leaned against a tree, and took careful aim. It was a long shot, even for a rifle, but he eased the trigger back. His rifle kicked and, to his joy, the stag dropped.

Behind them, the boys whooped, and Jacob looked over to the astonished face of Cicaho. But the brave did not waste any time with surprise, and led them all on a fast trot to the fallen deer. The poor creature was not yet dead, only incapacitated with a broken back, but that was quickly rectified.

It was a wonderful moment with everyone congratulating Jacob on his shot--everyone but Atotarho. Jacob glanced at him. *Why does he dislike me so?* Atotarho scowled, and looked away. Cicaho knelt, and began to expertly eviscerate the deer.

"Are you not proud of your father?" Jacob heard one of Shikellamy's sons ask.

"He is not my father!" Atotarho turned upon Jacob. "Look at him, a great white oaf. How could he be my father?"

"Silence," Cicaho roared. He had sprung to his feet, and was advancing upon Atotarho with his dripping knife. He pointed it at Atotarho's chest, and said venomously, "You shall not bring such dishonor upon your family."

Jacob was afraid. Cicaho had always impressed him with his nobility and wisdom, but that man was gone. In his place was a savage Iroquois with a knife . . . and he was angry. Who knew what he might do?

Jacob leaped before him, and pulled Atotarho behind himself. "He is my son! You shall not harm him."

Cicaho glared at him with his gory knife inches from Jacob's stomach. "Of course I shall not harm him." He stepped to one side, and said angrily to Atotarho, "But I shall inform your mother of your actions. You have brought great dishonor upon your entire family." He waved his knife dangerously close to the boy's face. "Your grandmother chose Techusin as your father. Who are you to despise him?" He turned upon his heel, and returned to the deer.

Atotarho yanked himself from Jacob's grasp, glared up at him for a moment, and then went to stand at the edge of the clearing by himself.

Jacob let him go, and stepped over to Shikellamy. In Algonquin, he asked, "Explain to me. Why was Cicaho so angry?"

The brave looked at him in surprise. "Your son dishonored you."

"I know that," Jacob said, "but it was dishonor to me alone. Why was Cicaho angry?"

"He did not only dishonor you. He also dishonored his grandmother and mother." Shikellamy shook his head sadly. "He has severely damaged your orenda, his own orenda, the orenda of us all." He looked at Jacob. "His actions have affected us all."

"Orenda?" Jacob asked. "I do not know this word."

"It is the spiritual force Teharonhiawagon, the maker, placed within each of us to resist the evil forces around us," Shikellamy explained patiently. "Do you not know that when you were adopted into your family your orenda was merged with theirs? That it made their orenda greater as well as their collective orendas increasing your own?" He grinned. "That was why your mother chose to adopt you; the orenda of a man who could leap from a cliff into a tree and survive must be mighty."

He grew sober. "But now Atotarho has dishonored you. That has damaged your orenda and his own. And in rejecting you, he has dishonored his mother and grandmother." He glanced at Atotarho and sighed. "Your family has lost much orenda." He looked back at Jacob, and said, "And your family's loss affects all within the village. We have all lost." He glanced to where Cicaho was angrily dividing the deer into roughly equal parts for the trip back to the village. "Do you now understand his anger?"

Jacob nodded soberly. He glanced at his son. He pitied the boy; Cicaho had threatened to inform his mother. One of the mysteries he was still trying to understand was the power women held among the Hodenosaunee. But though he did not completely understand it, he knew there was nothing even the bravest and boldest Hodenosaunee feared more than the displeasure of their mother. He wished he could spare his son that fate, but he did not know how.

Besides, he sighed, *he does not want my help. He would despise it just as he did my protecting him from Cicaho.*

He remembered his son's words, and almost laughed. The boy had accused him of being 'white'. He was sure that was not the true reason Atotarho rejected him; it was something far deeper. But one of the few thorns in his previous life in Berks County had been that there were some who had despised both him and Mateo because they were so 'brown'. It had been one of the things that had unified the two of them, and made it easy for people to accept that they were brothers; the fact that they were both noticeably more swarthy than most.

But now he was being rejected for being not brown enough.

Cicaho had finished dividing the meat, each man and boy shouldered his share, and the savage brave led the way back to the village. But instead of a happy trek anticipating a feast, it was a somber hike.

7 Be Someone's One?

September, 1771

Jacob stretched his back slowly. Was it his imagination, or did he hear it actually creak? It felt so good to finally stand straight again. It had been a long day, but the beans were finally picked. It was a bountiful harvest; his mother and sisters were pleased. But they had all come on at once so harvesting them had required everyone in the family, even little four-year-old Ailantha. Jacob looked at the corn and squash; it would not be long before they would be ready as well.

The Hodenosaunee called them the three sisters: beans, corn, and squash. They formed the basis of their diet; few meals did not include them in some form. But Sivathahae was very skilled; her meals were never monotonous, and always satisfying.

Jacob rubbed his lower back, but Melietha came and demanded he lie upon his stomach. When he obeyed, to his surprise, she stepped upon his back, and began to walk upon it. Although she was only eight, she was quite heavy, and this time his bones did not merely creak, they were popping rather loudly. But it felt very good, and he noticed little Ailantha was walking happily upon Atotarho's back. Jacob grinned at him, and received a rare grin in return.

The grin cheered him. Little things like that made him think there was still hope the boy would warm to him.

Unfortunately they still remained few and far between. Since his outburst in the forest, Atotarho had been scrupulously respectful and obedient, but he still displayed a cold disdain for Jacob. *It is too bad*, Jacob thought. *It would be so pleasant to spend my days with a son who likes me.* And despite the boy's disdain for him, Jacob liked him. He had learned that Atotarho had been very close to his former father who had died the summer before.

He cannot accept me as his replacement. I do not satisfy his concept of a man. Yet how can I when I do not understand Hodenosaunee men?

In many respects the Hodenosaunee men continued to be an enigma Jacob could not resolve. They had proven themselves to be every bit the savages he had always been warned they were yet, at the same time, they were perhaps the most noble men he had ever encountered.

Were they merely savages, I could understand them; not like them perhaps, but at least understand them.

He had expected such savage warriors to be brutes, ruled only by force and violence. Instead, he had found they were ruled by men chosen by their women, and disputes were settled peacefully by debate and oration. And they were exceedingly adept debaters and skilled orators.

The intelligence, the wisdom, the careful consideration and deliberation he had seen them display all seemed impossible to reconcile with their brutal savagery. How could he hope to be a man in his son's eyes if he found Hodenosaunee men so enigmatic?

Shall he ever accept me as I am? How can I make him realize I do not desire to, cannot hope to, replace his father, but that I can be another father if he shall but allow me?

Melietha had stopped walking on his back, and instead began to knead his back with her toes. Jacob closed his eyes, and allowed himself to revel in the bliss; she was a master.

He glanced at Atotarho. Ailantha was trying valiantly to imitate her sister, but it was clear the skill was yet beyond her. In fact, instead of the blissful face Jacob was sure he was displaying, Atotarho was struggling not to grimace. Jacob could not suppress a laugh at his distress. But he knew the boy would never let his little sister know he did not enjoy her ministrations, he cared far too much for her feelings to do that. That was perhaps the biggest reason Jacob could not help liking him: the affection and gentleness he displayed toward his little sisters.

Melietha stepped from him, and lay upon her stomach. "Now you do my back," she demanded.

Jacob sat up. "Me? But . . . I cannot walk on your back. I would crush you."

She laughed merrily. He loved to hear her laugh. "No, silly. You must use your hands." She pointed her chin at Atotarho and Ailantha.

Jacob saw that his son was on his knees straddling his sister's legs and was cracking her back with his hands. He hurried to imitate him. Soon Atotarho began to knead, and Jacob again did his best to copy his actions. But he could tell that although Melietha tried hard to hide the fact, he was at least as incompetent as Ailantha had been.

Atotarho had finished and was helping Ailantha to her feet before Jacob was finished with half of Melietha's back. He heard Ailantha beg her brother for a throw, and grinned to himself. There were two things he and Atotarho could count upon every time they returned from the forests: Melietha would run and leap into Jacob's arms demanding a hug, and Ailantha would run and leap into Atotarho's arms, and demand a throw.

Jacob laughed as he continued to massage Melietha's tight muscles. *That girl does love to be thrown.* And Jacob could tell Atotarho loved throwing her. But he sighed. Ailantha was growing . . . faster than Atotarho's strength was. *How long shall he continue to be able to throw her? It shall be a sad day for them both when he must admit he cannot.*

He decided he had done all he could for Melietha's back, and helped her to her feet.

She smiled up at him. "That was wonderful. You did a good job."

He laughed at her, and tucked the vagrant lock of her hair behind her ear. "You should not lie to your father!"

She laughed back, and Jacob heard Nehwahae, her friend ask, "Don't the white men massage each other's backs?" He had not heard her come up, but was not surprised, the two girls were rarely far separated.

"No," he admitted, "they do not." Not that he could remember at least.

"How about your mother's back?" he asked Melietha, "I'm sure she could use a massage." But Melietha giggled, and pointed her chin to where her mother was just then leaving with Dihanowich. Jacob sat, and watched them go. He had seen her disappear with Dihanowich before, but usually he did not come until much later in the evening.

"Where do they go together?" he asked.

To his surprise, Melietha did not answer, and he found both she and Nehwahae were blushing down at him.

"They . . . well, he is my mother's one."

"Your mother's . . . one?" Jacob felt like a fool, but he did not understand. "What does that mean?"

Melietha blushed a deeper bronze, but sank down to sit beside him, and whispered into his ear, "He is the one who is allowed to give her children."

"Give her . . ." He looked at the two girls. "You mean . . ." It was his turn to blush. Both girls burst out laughing at him.

For the first time Jacob noticed that both Atotarho and Melietha resembled Dihanowich; they shared his strong nose and cheekbones, and his grin. *So he is their true father.* He felt a strong pang of jealousy, but it quickly passed. *He may be their sire, but I am the one who is called their father. It is to me that Melietha runs, and my arms that she leaps into.* He looked again at Dihanowich's disappearing back. *It is he who should be jealous of me.*

But Dihanowich had never shown any particular interest in the two children; he had his own children, the children of his sisters.

Jacob still did not quite understand this odd situation, but discovering it had at least settled his mind in one regard. When he had been first adopted, and found he was the father of his sisters' children, he had wondered if the Hodenosaunee practiced incest. He had not seen how such a society could long survive, but did not see any other way to resolve the mystery. He had thought he would be expected to provide additional children, and worried how he would reconcile that duty with his religious scruples. Fortunately, his sisters had never approached him in that regard; he now understood why.

He was startled from his musing by Nehwahae demanding, "Why do you not become someone's one?" She smirked down upon him. "I know a couple of women who would be willing."

"Me!" Unbidden, the image of Hannah rose up before him. He shoved it away; it could never be. But he could not imagine siring children who would not be his own; he did not believe he could accept that.

But how could he explain that to the girls? This was their way. And he could tell this was a subject the girls would not let go. He was sure they could see the subject was embarrassing him, and that would be certain to motivate both of the little imps to continue to goad him. The girls were favorites of his, but they did love to tease.

Sure enough, Melietha giggled, and asked, "Yes. Why don't you?"

How can I turn it against them? Suddenly he knew.

He looked up into their smirking faces sadly, and said, "I can't."

"Why not?" The two girls had spoken in unison. They looked at each other, and laughed. But then Nehwahae looked back at Jacob, and again asked, "Why not?"

"Because," he said mournfully staring into her eyes, "you are far too young."

"Me?" she squealed.

"Yes. I am waiting for you." He reached out, and pulled her to his lap. "When you grow up, will you be my one?"

She squirmed away from him and stood, her cheeks a bright bronze. "No!"

Jacob shook his head mournfully. "You see? That is why I cannot be a one."

"Why?" the girls chorused.

"Every time I ask a girl to accept me, she always says, 'No'." He could no longer restrain his laughter, and ducked to ward off the pelting from small fists he knew was coming. But he suspected they would not continue to tease him about becoming someone's one.

8   fight for Meleitha

November, 1771

Jacob and Atotarho were returning from the forest. He had earned the trust and respect of his village and was now allowed free use of his weapons without being accompanied by other men and having his powder and shot doled out to him.

He caressed the smooth stock of his rifle. He had learned the Hodenosaunee, like many other Indians, gave their chief weapons names. He had called his rifle 'Hannah'. Using her name made him feel somehow still connected to her and the others he had lost.

It still hurt whenever he thought of them, but he knew they must be dead to him; he would almost certainly never again see them. Even if in some way Miranda's enmity were to cease and his notoriety throughout the colonies were to fade, he was now separated from Berks County by ten thousand Indians who would kill him on sight; he was now a Iroquois and would forever be a Iroquois in their minds. And neither Hannah nor Mateo would ever be welcomed by the Hodenosaunee, even if they desired to be.

'Iroquois' was their enemies' name for the Hodenosaunee, and not a nice name; it meant 'snake men' or 'brood of vipers'.   But Jacob found it amusing: Mr. Sablonski's nickname for him had used to be, 'Jake the Snake', now he was 'Techusin the Snake Man.' The nickname had proven oddly prophetic.

And while being an Iroquois had earned him the undying enmity of all Algonquin Indians, it had gained him the brotherhood of the Hodenosaunee, and Jacob had learned to value that brotherhood. As a

Seneca he was now a part of every other Hodenosaunee, and every other Hodenosaunee would seek his welfare. In most of the Six Nations he would be granted hospitality and friendship. Even in those nations, like the Cayugas, where he might not find welcome, he would find instant aid if attacked.

Having been virtually alone for most of his life, finding himself now a part of this vast brotherhood was intensely satisfying. Indeed, the village seemed more like one enormous family than any white settlement ever had. He was glad he was a part of it . . . of them. Everyone in the village seemed to accept and like him.

All but Atotarho; still, after all these months, he did not accept him.

God in Heaven, I pray you shall open his heart to me.
* * * *

Jacob and Atotarho arrived at the village and gave the prey they had obtained to Sivathahae.

"Rabbits," she exclaimed. "Three of them. Just what I was hoping for. And a duck. I think I shall trade it to Tehaowaxen for some herbs her son gathered." She called Ailantha to her.

But just then a young girl came screaming into the village. Jacob saw she was Nehwahae, Meleitha's best friend.

"A war party of Miami," she shrieked. "We were collecting nuts." She began to weep. "I do not know if anyone else escaped."

Sivathahae stared at Jacob in terror. "Melietha was with them."

Jacob ran with several other men to Nehwahae. Jacob was glad to see Cicaho was among them.

The girl pointed to the southwest in reply to Cicaho's questions. "There were seven. No, they were not painted. They . . . they . . ." She was struggling hard not to cry.

Jacob squatted beside her, and put his hand on her arm. She threw her arms around him, buried her face in his shoulder, and wept.

Jacob held her, and Cicaho told the two other men who had assembled to arm themselves; he and Jacob were both already armed. Nehwahae regained control of herself, and Jacob gently pushed her away, but kept both hands on her shoulders. Cicaho squatted beside them.

"Which way did they go?" he asked gently.

Nehwahae did not take her eyes from Jacob's, but answered Cicaho, "To the south."

"How many girls did they take?"

She shook her head, and struggled for a moment before she could answer. "I do not know. I ran."

Cicaho reached out, and rubbed her back. "It is good that you did run. You did the right thing." He paused for a moment. "How many girls were with you?"

"Seven. That is, there were seven of us, so six." She finally looked at Cicaho. "There were six with me."

Cicaho nodded, and stood. "You did well. Go to your mother." Nehwahae ran. The two other braves were returning.

Two women had appeared, one with a small pot of paint, and the other with a bowl of what smelled to Jacob like goose grease. Cicaho and the others dipped their fingers, and quickly painted their faces with fearsome streaks. Jacob had never worn paint but followed their example.

Then the braves each removed his skull cap and, dipping his fingers in the grease, ran it through his hair so it stood up on end. Since the men wore their caps except when bathing, Jacob had almost forgotten that many of them had only a ridge of hair running across their scalp; all of the rest of their scalp had been plucked free of hair. Now their ridge of hair stood flared, and the braves had been transformed in an instant into dreadful Iroquois warriors. They were a fearsome sight indeed, but one which now Jacob found comforting. He removed his own cap, but did not grease his hair; it was much too long.

He glanced back at his sister and son. He saw rage, fear, and naked desire in Atotarho's face. *Melietha is his sister. It must be killing him to be left behind.* Without another thought he lifted his chin, and called, "Come."

The boy came with fear and determination battling upon his face. He hesitated when he came to the pot of paint, and glanced up at Jacob who nodded, and the boy dipped his fingers reverently and streaked his face. When he was done, he gave Jacob a glance that Jacob for a moment mistook for adoration. *It could not have been. He has made his feelings regarding me clear. It is amazing how a few streaks of paint can alter one's appearance.*

Cicaho nodded at them, and led them all on a fast lope from the village.

They soon found the glade where the girls had been collecting nuts and, with hardly a moment's hesitation, turned to follow the party's trail. Jacob believed himself to be an excellent tracker, but he had difficulty discerning the minute traces left by the party while he was at a full run. Clearly Cicaho did not.

Within minutes, Cicaho slowed his pace, and held up a hand. Jacob and the rest gathered beside him.

"They are just ahead," the brave said. "I do not wish to reveal ourselves to them." "Techusin," he said to Jacob, "take your son and flank them on their left." He commanded another man to flank their right and the third to remain on their rear. "I shall circle them until I am in their front. Let no one reveal himself until you hear my cry."

Jacob and the other men nodded and broke away to their respective assignments. Jacob could easily discern where their quarry was. Taking care to discover any out rangers they may have, he led his son to their left flank. He found the party had no out rangers; they were traveling in a group at little more than a fast trot. They entered and began to cross a small clearing and Jacob was forced to widen his distance to remain concealed, but he got his first good view of them.

There were seven men surrounding five girls.

Nehwahae said there were six girls with her, so either one of them also escaped capture, or one is dead. His anger rose. *There had better not be one dead.*

One of the Miami was following the girls with a sharp stick which he used to prod any girl who faltered or failed to maintain the pace set for them. Meleitha's back was bleeding from several wounds, and Jacob's wrath boiled. He had to restrain himself from shooting the brute abusing her, but he could not reveal himself until Cicaho's signal.

But then the air was rent by Cicaho's war cry which was answered immediately from the right and rear. Jacob also screamed as he cocked Hannah, slid her to his cheek, and squeezed the trigger. The man following Melietha fell without a sound as the others froze in their tracks.

Jacob thrust Hannah into Atotarho's hands and dropped his horn and shot bag at his feet. "Stay in the brush. But reload and use her." Several other shots rang out, but he gave them no heed, chose the largest of their foes, drew his tomahawk, and charged.

Unfortunately their surprise had expired, and the man met his charge. In the violent parrying which ensued Jacob could get no advantage for several desperate moments, but his bloodlust grew. He saw and heard nothing but his opponent, and nothing mattered but his death. He saw an opening and struck, disemboweling him. At almost the same instant, a shot rang out which Jacob recognized to be Hannah's and the next moment he was bowled over from the rear and driven upon his groaning victim. He rolled free, saw his foe was yet alive, and dashed his brains out.

He saw he had been tackled by the corpse of another enemy which now lay bleeding from a neat hole in its temple; Atotarho had shot him. Jacob was impressed; that had been an exceedingly good shot at a moving target. He was proud of the boy. But there was no time to waste; he dashed to where a comrade was wrestling with a foe, and his tomahawk struck for a third time.

The battle was over; all seven of their foes were dead. Jacob was dismayed to see one of their own, K'soawatha, was also dead.

Then with a wrenching of his gut he spied the second man he had killed: a bloody abomination with gore splayed all about him. Jacob very nearly vomited. He had killed three men; three men were dead because of him. He had never thought of himself as a killer, never even imagined using Hannah to take another man's life. Now he had not only killed, but killed passionately, brutally, and savagely.

But then he heard his daughter call his name. He ran to her, sliced the cord which bound her arms, and was engulfed in them.

"I knew you would come for me," she cried. "I knew it."

She winced as his hands brushed one of her wounds, and his wrath again boiled. He no longer cared that he had killed those men, nor how he had done so. He had only done what he had had to do to rescue his daughter and the other girls. He saw Atotarho out of the corner of his eye, passed Melietha to him, and took back his rifle.

He watched the two embrace; he enjoyed the sight. *The Hodenosaunee are exceedingly passionate warriors, but are equally passionate in their affection for each other.*

He waited until Atotarho released his sister, and then put his hand upon his shoulder. "That was an exceptional shot you made. You saved my life. Thank you." He was unsure what else to say. After an awkward pause, he added, "I'm proud of you."

The boy glanced up, and grinned at him. With a rush of emotion Jacob realized Atotarho finally accepted him. He wanted to sweep the boy up in an embrace, but knew he would find such a display before the other warriors offensive. Instead he pulled out his knife and handed it to him. Pointing at the man the boy had shot he said, "Take his scalp. A man should keep his first kill."

The Indian practice of taking their enemies' scalps as a trophy had always repulsed Jacob; it had been one of many things he had not been able to understand about them. But it now seemed appropriate, and certainly his son deserved to do so.

Atotarho hurried to obey, and soon returned the bloody knife. "Now take your own," he said.

Jacob did not want to take the scalps of his victims, but his comrades had already taken their own and were waiting for him to do the same. He knew they would not understand his reluctance, so he forced himself to do so. He took them in the reverse order of their deaths.

The first was disgusting, the second routine, and the third exhilarating.

So quickly is the veneer of civilization stripped away to reveal the savage I truly am.

But he did not care; he accepted his savagery. The third was the scalp of the man who had bloodied his daughter's back. He glanced at her and was rewarded by the satisfied requital in her face. He thrust the dripping scalps to the sky, and screamed his exaltation. The scream was echoed by the other warriors.

By then they had been joined by half a dozen other men from the village. Jacob was relieved to hear the missing girl had returned and was safe. A bier was quickly fashioned and the fallen Hodenosaunee was respectfully placed upon it, and borne to his family.

But before they left the scene of the battle, the heart was ripped from each enemy corpse. Jacob worried why they were doing so. He hoped they did not intend to eat them. Would God forgive him if he participated in such a feast? But could he avoid doing so?

That night he participated with the other warriors in a wild war dance around the fire. The beat of the drums and the rhythms of the dance were intoxicating; he felt himself being drawn into them, becoming one with the other warriors, and he yielded to them. He was a Hodenosaunee warrior, both the noble man and the vicious savage. Both dwelt within him and no longer seemed incongruous. He embraced them both.

The virgins of the tribe paraded out wearing only their ritual feathers and ribbons and wove their way among and between the men. Several stopped to dance before Jacob. He knew they were inviting him to visit their longhouse and ask their mother for permission to become their one. He had gained great honor that day.

The sight of their naked dancing bodies drove him wild with desire; one especially was enticing. The savage within him lusted to sate its desire, but the nobleman remembered clear grey eyes which could see into the depths of his soul. He knew he would almost certainly never again see them; why should the memory of Hannah restrain him?

But it did not matter, for her memory had restrained him. The allure of the dancing girls faded like the imaginations of a fevered mind. *When one has lost a lustrous pearl, even the most lovely glass bead can not suffice.* Though beautiful, none of these women had earned his love.

Then one of the 'old women' appeared with a large platter bearing the hearts of their foes. The dance stopped, and the men parted to allow her to carry it into their midst.

This is it; now is when I must decide, do I eat, or do I not.

But, to his relief, the two white dogs which were being groomed for the spring festival were led forth and fed the hearts. In this way, he realized, the entire village would eat the men's hearts for the dogs ate them, and soon the villagers would eat the dogs.

The rejoicing and the honor he had gained were pleasant, but he was glad when it was over and he could return to the peace of his family's longhouse.

Outside the door he found Ailantha begging Atotarho for a throw.

"You have not thrown me all day," she accused. "Won't you please throw me now?"

Atotarho glanced at Jacob, and then said, "You should ask Techusin to throw you. He is much stronger than I."

Ailantha looked at Jacob uncertainly, but her brother gave her a shove. "Go on."

She came, and Jacob threw her up into the air. She squealed and laughed, and hardly had he caught her when she demanded, "Again." He threw her a second time.

"Again," she demanded, but he laughed at her, and set her down.

"Tomorrow," he promised, and led her into the longhouse.

He unrolled his sleeping mat, but saw Atotarho sitting upon his own mat watching him. Jacob knew what it had likely cost the boy to send Ailantha to him to throw.

Among the Hodenosaunee, the place beside a father's mat was reserved for the child he wished to honor. Jacob had several times before offered it to Atotarho, but the boy had always disdained to accept it. This time, when he patted the floor beside him, he was rewarded by a smile, and the boy gathered his mat, and came to him.

Here, within the longhouse, Jacob was sure the boy would not find a show of affection offensive, and he held out his arms. As they embraced, Jacob had to struggle to restrain his tears.

Atotarho was finally his true son.

9   A Bear Forever?

November, 1771

Jacob could not sleep. Ever since he had assisted in recovering the girls, he had been acknowledged as a warrior. Not only had this meant Atotarho finally accepted him, it had granted him a good deal of status and an increase in his orenda.

However, it was the habit of Hodenosaunee warriors to pluck their hair leaving only a three or four inch fringe atop their scalp running from front to back. And Jacob found himself very reluctant to do so. Yet he did not know why.

It was not the pain of plucking his hair; already he had allowed Melietha to pluck his facial hair. She seemed to get a sadistic pleasure doing so and now complained that it no longer grew. It was true: his facial hair had never been thick, but it had become very sparse.

And it was not that he found the almost bald heads of the warriors offensive, he actually found them quite noble. So why did he have this strange reluctance to pluck his hair?

He did not know; he only knewknew he did not want to.

Ailantha's whimper broke into his thoughts. She often awoke from bad dreams. He heard her mother, Sivathahae, sit up and try to comfort her.

"I dreamed the bears had come for me, and wouldn't let me go," Jacob heard Ailantha whisper.

"S-h-h. You see it was only a dream, there are no bears here."

"But," Ailantha protested, "what if they do come?"

Jacob felt guilty. This dream was his fault.

There were few things the Hodenosaunee, children or adults, liked more than telling and listening to stories, and they had found Jacob was an excellent story teller. Not only did he have a wealth of stories from his youth in Europe and from the Bible, but he knew of many imaginary creatures of which they had never heard: fairies and elves, brownies and giants, trolls, dwarfs, and ogres.

Nearly every evening, the children of his longhouse would beg him for a story, so he always tried to make up an exciting one during the day. He enjoyed doing so.

That evening he had told the children of a girl, Heinike, who had been captured by a family of bears who treated her very nicely because they wanted a pretty little girl for their own. They were so kind that she was very happy and eventually stopped missing her human friends and family. She no longer wished to leave the bears. But then the bears asked her to drink a potion which would change her into a bear.

And, although Heinike was happy with the bears and did not wish to leave them, she did not want to become a bear. She knew that if she became a bear, she would never be able to return to her human village. While she was not anxious to return, deep down, she hoped to return someday.

So in the end she found a way to escape the bears and run back to her village where she could remain a girl.

I guess I made the story a little too exciting.

Jacob rose and crossed to where Sivathahae was holding Ailantha. "I'm sorry I frightened her," he whispered.

"No," his sister said, "your stories are wonderful. Do not change them."

Jacob held out his arms to Ailantha, and she crawled from her mother's lap to his own. "Ailantha, you know it was only a story, don't you? The bears shall not come for you."

She looked up at him soberly. "But what if they do?"

"I will not let them. If they try to take you, I shall follow them and get you back." He hugged her tightly. "You are my little girl, and I will not allow anyone to take you away, not even a bear."

"Just like you went after Melietha?"

"Just like I went after Melietha."

She ran her hand over his bicep. "And you are very strong."

He had to struggle to stifle a laugh. He knew it was important to her. "Yes. I am very strong. And I shall always come for you. I shall never allow anyone to take you away."

She snuggled against his shoulder contentedly.

"Do you think you can sleep now?"

She nodded, and he tried to lay her back upon her pad. But when he did, she clung to him. "U-u-ngh. Do not leave me!"

"But . . ." Jacob was unsure what to do or say. He did not feel comfortable sleeping next to Ailantha with Sivathahae on the other side of her. Despite the fact that she was his sister . . . it did not seem appropriate.

"Take her with you," Sivathahae suggested.

"Are you sure?" Jacob was surprised. Ailantha had always slept next to her mother.

"Yes," she said. "It is time she stops spending all her time with me." She picked up Ailanta's pad, and put it at the head of Jacob's. "Here you go, Ailantha. You can sleep near Techusin. Then if you feel afraid, you shall be able to reach out and touch his hair or head and know you are safe."

Jacob lay down, and so did Ailantha. She stared at him soberly, smiled, and curled up. Jacob soon heard her breathing slow and deepen. He leaned upon his elbows, and stared at her.

He found her trust in him endearing. He saw she had a lock of her hair in her mouth. He laughed, and tried to remove it, but, even in her sleep, she clung quite tenaciously to it, and he left it be. It made her look innocent and helpless and magnified his desire to protect her.

He lay back, glad she was his daughter and happy he had the honor of protecting and serving her.

But he still could not sleep. The story he had told of Heineke was bothering him. Somehow it seemed more than just a story.

Then he realized the truth: the story was his story; he was Heineke.

He, like she, was very contented among his captors, did not desire to leave them. But like she, he deep down, so deep he had not, until that very moment, known it was true, hoped to someday return to his previous life.

He could not imagine ever choosing to leave his children, his family, the Hodenosaunee people, and if he did, there would remain Miranda to deal with. Still, the possibility of a return remained.

But if he plucked his head, it would not be long before the hair would cease to grow. He would then be forever easily identified as an Iroquois, and as such, would be unwelcome in any Algonquin Indian or white settlement. He was not sure if even Hannah herself would accept him. That was why he did not want to pluck his head; he would then forever be unable to return to Hannah and Mateo and his other white friends.

With a start, the name Heineke forced itself to the forefront of his consciousness. *Heineke. Why did I name the girl in my story Heineke?* He usually named his heroes or heroines after his children, their cousins, or friends. The children always especially enjoyed a story of someone with their own name. But Heineke was not a Hodenosaunee name; it was a Jewish name.

It was his sister's name.

He had not thought of her in years. She would be . . . he had to do the math . . . nineteen. He felt like weeping. His sister, whom he had last seen when she was six, was a woman, maybe married with children. He wondered what she was like, what his perhaps brother-in-law was like.

The image of his little sister as a young woman standing beside a handsome Jewish man rose up before him. He knew it was only his imagination of what they would look like; he would never see the reality. But his imaginary image of his possible brother-in-law filled him with shame. He saw the long locks of hair hanging far down his shoulders, the locks before his ears which had never been cut, which immediately identified him as a Jew.

Jacob's father and grandfather had had those locks, so once had Jacob, but almost the first thing which had been done to him aboard the ship to America, had been to cut those locks off. The captain had not wanted him to be identifiable as a Jew.

Jacob, even when he had gained his freedom, had never regrown them. The closest he had come had been to allow all of his hair to grow and tie it at the nape of his neck. But he knew that had been more to imitate Mr. Wallace, his master, than to adhere to the Jewish laws and traditions.

He felt ashamed of himself. *That was why I chose the name Heineke, to remind myself I am a Jew.*

It was another reason, an important reason, why he could not pluck his hair. Were he to do so, how could he ever again identify himself as a Jew?

But how can I explain to my Hodenosaunee family and friends that I do not wish to pluck my hair because it would make it impossible to ever again return to my white family or again be a Jew? How could I make them understand?

He knew he could not explain his hope to someday return to Hannah and Mateo, not without risking offending them.

But I do not have to explain that I wish to be identified as a Jew. They already know I am a Jew and desire to remain one. And while I have not, strictly speaking, kept the law regarding my hair, they do not know that.

He had not cut his hair since coming to them. He need only inform them of the law, he felt sure they would accept it as a valid reason for not plucking his head. The Hodenosaunee were very accommodating of other's religious beliefs.

He felt something in his hair. He almost leaped up and swatted whatever it was away before he realized it was Ailantha's small hand. She had awakened and, following her mother's advice, was feeling his hair to reassure herself of his presence. She seemed to enjoy doing so, for the hand progressed down to caress his cheek, then his nose, and finally his mouth and chin. It then returned to his hair where it played with it, combing through it and winding it around a finger.

Jacob found the strange sensations quite relaxing. His troubles seeped away, and he slept.

10 Musket Repair

October, 1773

Jacob moved slowly through the forest with Cicaho's two sons keeping pace some hundred feet upon his left and Atotarho upon his right. Glimpses of the enormous buck they were herding caused him to lick his lips in anticipation. They were nearly to the copse where he knew Cicaho waited. Being invited to hunt with Cicaho was a great honor; an honor Jacob now often enjoyed.

Any moment the shot would ring which would fell the deer and ensure a feast. Both families would eat well that night as well as many friends and an ample supply of dried and smoked meat would be added to that already hanging from their longhouse ceiling.

But the copse was reached and Jacob watched in dismay as the buck ambled past it.

Shoot, Cicaho, surely *you must see it. Why does he not shoot?*

Jacob had to fight the urge to cock Hannah and shoot the buck himself but, although he believed Cicaho to be in the copse, he could not be certain. He could not take the chance of him being in the line of fire.

The buck escaped, and Jacob and the boys jogged to the copse and found a wrathful Cicaho awaiting them.

"Why did you not shoot?" asked Cicaho's oldest son, Aikyla.

"I did shoot," Cicaho raged, "but this . . ." He released a string of invectives. ". . . musket failed to fire."

Atotarho caught Jacob's eye, and grinned up at him. Jacob had to struggle not to grin back. Both he and his son respected Cicaho, but the man did have a temper and when he was unable to vent his anger, his frustration could be amusing to watch. Just now it was clear he desired to dash his weapon against the nearest tree, but one does not abuse even a musket so.

But Cicaho had noticed the grin and, to Jacob's relief, grinned back. He sighed angrily and scowled at his gun. "It has been doing so more and more of late. It is becoming nearly useless."

"Let me see it," Jacob asked, and handed Hannah to Atotarho.

Cicaho handed it over without a word, and Jacob inspected it. He easily saw what the problem was: the pivot of the flintlock was made of brass. With use the soft metal had worn resulting in an enormous degree of play in the motion of the flint. It was now very easy for the flint to miss its mark and so not spark; no spark and there would be no fire.

Why did anyone make a musket using brass for the flintlock pivot? They had to know it should be steel; surely substituting brass could not have saved much cost.

The question was: could he repair it? The only permanent repair would be to replace the brass pivot with one of steel, but that was impossible. But, if he took care, Jacob believed he could peen the brass enough to realign the flint. It would of course not be a permanent repair, but it would work for a time. He regarded Cicaho.

"I think I may be able to repair it," he said. "But I cannot be sure. Do you trust me to try?"

Cicaho considered him skeptically, but nodded.

Jacob first carefully fired the gun; he was not about to peen the brass with a charge of gunpowder inches away. He had to fire it twice before it sparked and fired. He then searched for and found a large flat rock to use as an anvil. He wished he had a true hammer, but the back of his tomahawk would have to suffice.

Atotarho knelt by his side watching. Jacob explained what he was going to try to do. "I must go slow and easy though. I can always peen the pivot more, but if I peen it too much, I cannot unpeen it." He increased the force of his blows until the metal began to yield. Then he had to take care not to misalign the flint. Several times he stopped and tested the action. Finally he was satisfied, and handed the musket back to its owner.

Cicaho's face looked worried. Jacob could imagine what he had thought as he had watched him beat upon his gun with the back of a tomahawk. But when the brave tested the action of the flint, his frown changed to a grin.

"It's as good as new." He held out the musket to his sons, and said, "Look at what Techusin did."

But Cicaho's younger son, Hysora, whispered, "Shh. Father, the buck is back." He pointed into the brush.

Everyone sank down, and followed his finger.

"Techusin," Cicaho asked quietly, "It's a long shot. Do you think your Hannah could reach him?"

Cicaho had learned Hannah could reach further than his musket, and of course his musket was not loaded.

"I'm sure she can," said Jacob. "Atotarho, take him."

"But . . .," the boy protested, and held out Hannah to him.

"There is no time," Jacob whispered. "Quickly, take him while you may."

He watched with pride as Atotarho cocked Hannah, slid her to his cheek, and fired. The stag dropped, and lay still.

Jacob could tell Cicaho was impressed, but the man merely grinned at Atotarho, and then ran to bleed the carcass. Jacob did not want to embarrass his son by commending him before Cicaho's sons, but squeezed his shoulder as he took back his rifle. He knew Atotarho would understand.

* * * *

"Techusin!"

Melietha had seen them as soon as they had come through the gate of the palisade, and came running. But she was unable to leap into Jacob's arms as was her norm for he was laden with parts of the buck; instead she danced about them like a nymph admiring their catch and talking so fast Jacob could hardly hear it all.

He glanced at Atotarho laden with his own share of the meat. Most boys would be boasting about the buck by now, but his son was saying not a word. *Two years I've known the boy, and he is still surprising and impressing me.* Cicaho caught his eye, and Jacob could see he was also impressed by the boy.

Yet, although the boy was too dignified to tell of his shot himself, Jacob believed he desired to have his friends know, so when he dropped his load at his sister's feet, and Melietha leaped into his arms as he knew she would, he whispered into her ear that Atotarho had shot the buck all by himself. She was not slow in spreading the news; she was very fond of her brother and glad for an opportunity to brag about him.

Jacob glanced at Atotarho's face, and saw he had been right; the boy was happy the tale was being told even though he could not have told it himself. Jacob grinned.

What else are little sisters good for?

At that moment Ailantha came running on her lithe little legs. Jacob knew what she wanted; she wanted to be thrown. Jacob humored her but, as he swept her up, caught Cicaho's eye and threw her so instead of flying straight up as she expected, she flew away to fall into Cicaho's arms. Her scream and her face as she found herself sailing away from him made both men laugh, but as soon as she found herself safely back upon the ground, she ran back to demand he do it again.

Jacob sat upon the ground, Ailantha crawled upon his lap, and he surveyed the scene before him with joy. His remarkable son, his two delightful and lovely daughters, his sister already preparing a portion of the buck for a sumptuous feast, and his good friend, Cicaho.

Could life be any better than this?

He hugged Ailantha, and she giggled and asked, "What was that for?"

"Just because I love you."

11   Injin Smith

October, 1773

By morning the news that Jacob could repair muskets had spread throughout the village; everyone began bringing him their weapons. To Jacob's surprise he found Cicaho's musket was typical of them all; every one had a brass pivot. It was mystifying.

It was also frustrating. While he could return a musket to reliable working order, he knew his repairs were at best temporary and he doubted he would be able to repair them a second time.

Nonetheless, although he was frankly honest with all who came, his repairs were very popular. Within a few weeks visitors were coming from many miles around. Jacob could hardly keep up with the work; he taught Atotarho to help him. Since everyone brought a gift to pay them for their labor, his family did not suffer from his lack of hunting.

"But," he said to the chief of the village, "I feel guilty making repairs which I know are only temporary. Why do all the muskets have brass pivots?"

"All of our muskets were obtained from the English traders," answered the chief. "They are as they have always been."

Jacob struggled to restrain his anger. "Perhaps it is time we obtain new traders. The ones we have appear to be cheating us."

But the chief shook his head. "The English are our allies. We must use the traders approved by them. The Seneca have agreed to do so as a part of the terms of our alliance."

"Then we must speak to the English. They must be informed of their representatives' actions."

The chief considered him for several moments, and then said, "We must first speak with a sachem. Only the sachems may negotiate with the English." He thought for a few moments, and then nodded. "I shall send word we need to consult with one."

* * * *

"Every musket the Seneca have purchased from the English traders is defective," Jacob told the sachem. "They are designed to fail early. I believe I can repair them, but I shall need steel pivots to replace these brass ones."

"Where could such pivots be obtained?" asked the sachem.

Jacob was a little in awe of the great man; there were only eight sachems in the entire Seneca Nation. They it were who represented the nation at the great council fire of the Hodenosaunee where matters pertaining to all the Six Nations were decided.

"Any good gunsmith should be able to supply them." Jacob eyed the sachem; should he tell him of his suspicions? "I do not know why whoever made these muskets used brass in the first place."

The sachem's face hardened. "I suspect I know why. They shall make them so no longer." He worked the flint speculatively. "What else do you find wrong with these muskets?"

Jacob thought for a moment. Other than being of clearly inferior and cheap workmanship, he had found nothing else amiss and told the sachem as much.

The sachem thrust the musket into Jacob's hands. "You shall receive your steel pivots. In the meantime, make the repairs the best you can."

He turned upon his heel and departed.

* * * *

The sachem did not return for more than a month and, when he did, was accompanied by a rare English visitor and they

53

did not come to Jacob, but went to confer with the village chief. The entire village knew of their arrival and anxiously awaited word of its portent.

By and by word was sent to summon Jacob's mother and the 'old woman' of their longhouse. When they emerged their faces were stoic and sad. They ordered their families to attend them and went directly to their longhouse. Everyone, even the smallest child, filed in silently and took their places around the central fire facing the 'old woman' where she sat on her mat.

She sat silent for several long minutes but all could see she was gazing sadly at Jacob and his family. Finally she addressed him.

"Techusin, the English have come to the sachems of the Seneca and demanded they no longer allow you to live among us."

There was a very audible gasp from many of group and Jacob felt as though he had been punched in the gut; he was unable to breathe.

"Why?" he finally managed to ask. "Are there not other white men who have been adopted into the tribe?"

"There are others."

"Shall they also be sent away?"

"No." She held up her hand to stop the obvious question to follow. "I do not know why they selected only you; they would not tell me. Presumably they told the sachems, but perhaps not. I know only they demand the Senecas drive you from our midst and forbid your return." She stopped and stared at her hands clenched in her lap before adding, "And our sachems have agreed."

She eyed Jacob. "We cannot jeopardize our alliance with the English. Even if we do not understand why they have made this demand, it is a price we cannot afford not to pay."

Every eye was sympathetically focused on Jacob and he nodded. "I understand."

The 'old woman' nodded also and said, "The Englishman is here to escort you from our lands. He shall take you as soon as you have said your goodbyes." She looked away and struggled to regain her composure. When she had, she looked back at him and said, "You shall be forbidden to ever again enter any of the lands of the Six Nations. To do so would bring great dishonor upon us all and threaten our alliance with the English. Do you understand?"

"I do."

She sighed and said, "Very well then, we shall leave you with your family until you have said your goodbyes. You may then send for who ever else with whom you would wish to speak and then you shall be taken."

"Taken. You mean bound?"

"No." Her chin rose. "We have been assured you shall be treated with the utmost respect and set at your liberty as soon as you leave Hodenosaunee lands. Cicaho shall accompany you to ensure the Englishman does so."

Cicaho. Jacob could think of no one he would prefer to accompany him. The 'old woman' pointed her chin at the door and all but Jacob's immediate family exited but not before many expressed their condolences and ire to Jacob concerning his fate.

12   Exiled again

January, 1774

Jacob sat and stared at the floor. *How do you say goodbye forever to those you love?*

It was his third time; if anyone should be an expert, it should be he but his past experiences gave him no clue how to handle this one.

Why does God keep giving me people to love only to rip me away? Why am I so cursed?

But the time for such thoughts was not now. His family was awaiting him. He looked first to Atotarho, his son and eldest child. But he did not know what to say or do.

He finally went to squat before him. Taking his tomahawk from his belt, he offered it. It was the valuable North Carolina tomahawk he had gotten from Dave at the shoot.

"I want you to have it. And I want your tomahawk." Atotarho had received his tomahawk right after he had gone on the rescue party with Jacob; as a proven warrior, he had a right to be armed. He was never without it, but it was only a cheap trader tomahawk.

The Hodenosaunee, like many Indians, believed a man's weapons absorbed a bit of his soul which would become a part of the weapon.

"I want my soul to remain with you, and for your soul to accompany me."

Atotarho gazed into his eyes, the faintest glimmer of a smile passed over his features and was gone. He pulled out his own tomahawk, and the exchange was made. He then jumped up, and began to run from the longhouse.

Jacob called him back. The Jews believed a father could bless or curse a son and their words would come to pass. Jacob desired to bless Atotarho.

"God of heaven and earth," he prayed silently as the boy returned to face him, "hear my prayer. Recognize Atotarho as my true son and I as his true father."

He pushed the boy to his knees before him. He eyed him for a long moment and then said, "Atotarho, you shall be a great man; a mighty man; a leader remembered among your people." The words seemed to flow from his mouth without his conscious thought; he believed they were a true blessing.

He then leaned close to his son, and whispered, "And I shall forever be proud to call you my son; my son whom I love."

Atotarho's face wavered, but then became stoic.

He has the most innate dignity of anyone I have ever known, man or boy. God in heaven, how I thank you for allowing me to call him my son.

Atotarho walked slowly to the door of the longhouse. There was one brief instant when he turned and glanced back, and then he was gone.

Gone. Like everyone else I have ever loved. Why God? Why does this keep happening to me?

But Jacob pushed those thoughts aside, and turned his attention to his daughters. Tears were streaming down both of their lovely faces. He went to them, dropped to his knees, and held out his arms; they flew into them. For the last time he held them, told them how very much he loved them, how proud he was of them. He never wanted to release them, but the time came when it seemed right to do so, and he did.

Their tears had ceased, and they stood staring soberly into his eyes. He wished he could leave a bit of his soul with them, and take a bit of theirs as he had their brother, but how could he do so?

Ailantha reached out and traced his eyebrows. She had always loved to feel his face. He reached out and traced the shape of her nose and lips. Suddenly they were both tracing each other's face almost frantically until they were both giggling too hard to continue.

He turned to Melietha. Of the three children, he believed he would most miss her. It had been she who had first welcomed him into the family, she who continued to welcome him whenever he returned to her. It had been she who had broken through his natural reserve and taught him to express his affection freely and exuberantly.

He saw the lock of hair which had always been her bane again dangling in her face; it always seemed determined to escape the rest of her hair. He gently tucked it behind her ear, and then cradled her chin in his hand.

"How shall I live," he asked quietly, "without my Melietha calling my name, and leaping into my arms whenever I return home?"

She stared at him mutely, and he drew her to him, kissed her right in the middle of her forehead, and whispered, "Oh, how I love you." He stood abruptly, and turned to his sisters.

He did not know what to say to them. Although he liked and respected them, he had never established a real relationship with them; they felt more like coworkers than relatives. Fortunately his elder sister saved him by thanking him warmly for being such a good provider, and for loving her children as he had.

His younger sister echoed her sentiments, but then threw her arms around him, kissed him full upon the lips, and whispered in his ear, "But you do not know how often I have wished you were not my brother, and how jealous I was of Melietha when she would snuggle with you." She flashed him a wicked smirk, and stepped back.

Jacob could only stand and watch her. She had been right; he had not known, had not even suspected. His eyes involuntarily swept over her body. It was just as well he had not suspected; she was a very attractive woman.

He turned away from her, and focused upon the matriarch of the family. Although she was his adopted mother, she had never felt like it. Of all of his Hodenosaunee family, she was the most distant. Yet he did esteem and respect her; liked her. He again did not know what to say, but finally said, "I thank you for adopting me as your son, making me a brother to your daughters, and a father to your grandchildren. You honored me greatly."

She held out her arms, he went to her, and she embraced him warmly. He was surprised; he had not suspected she had had such affection for him. She released him, but kept her hands upon his shoulders to say, "We may have to send you away, forbidding you to return, but you shall not cease to be a part of my family." She glanced in the direction of the village council house, raised her chin proudly, and then eyed him. "Men cannot expel a member from a family, only a mother can, and I do not. Our orenda shall remain with you, and yours with us."

"You honor me greatly," he told her, and meant it. "You are a great family and your orenda is strong."

She released him, and he looked around at each one of his family one last time. He did not want to leave them. His arms ached to hug them again, especially his children.

He forced himself instead to gather together his ammunition and a few other items, roll them into a blanket to form a pack, take up his rifle, and stride to the door. But at the door he stopped struck by an inspiration. He dropped his pack, leaned Hannah against the wall, and returned to where his daughters were standing hand in hand watching him.

Again he knelt before them. Taking out his knife, he addressed Melietha. "May I cut off the lock of hair which always falls into your face?" Already it had escaped her ear and was obscuring her left eye. She nodded, and he cut it off leaving several inches so its loss would not be too noticeable.

Turning to Ailantha, he asked, "May I cut off the lock you suck upon at night?" He laughed at her expression; at five, she was rather old to have retained such a habit. "You didn't think I knew you suck upon it, did you?"

She shook her head.

He reached out, and gently separated it from the rest of her hair. "This is it, is it not?" When she nodded, he asked, "May I have it?" When she again nodded, he cut it off.

He then carefully cut a lock from the long hair which hung before each of his ears. He knew his family knew the importance of those locks; that they were sacred to him, and had never before been cut. He laid them before the girls, and carried their locks to his elder sister and asked her to braid them into the hair in front of each ear. Without his even needing to ask her, his younger sister went and braided his locks into each of the girl's hair.

When they were done, he stared at his daughters one last time, and smiled. The brown of his locks stood out boldly against the black of theirs. He was pleased.

It is good. I shall leave a bit of myself with them, and take a bit of them with me.

He swore to himself he would never allow their hair to be parted from him.

He turned toward the door, but his mother called him back.

"Is there no one else in the village with whom you would wish to speak? We shall leave you, and call them in."

Jacob considered it. There were many who were his good friends. He wished he could express what they each had meant to him, but he did not know how, and did not trust himself to control his emotions any further. He believed his friends already knew his feelings. Yet there was one with which he wished to speak in private.

"Send me the sachem."

He could tell his mother was surprised at his choice, but she led the way out of the longhouse, and the rest of the family followed her. The sachem was not long in coming.

"Tell me," Jacob demanded, "why the English wish me exiled."

"I cannot. They did not give us a reason." He eyed Jacob. "You must realize when allies meet, reasons for demands are often not given. Each side makes their demands, and those demands are negotiated until an agreement is reached."

"The Seneca received something in return for accepting this demand?"

"You may be sure we did."

"Then the English," stated Jacob, "desired my absence with some urgency. Why do you think that is?"

The sachem considered him, and then asked, "Why do you think it is?"

"I think the English knew your muskets were faulty; they designed them to be. They wanted them to wear out. Now that you have discovered the pivots are brass and demand replacements, they shall supply them, but they hope to supply you with pivots made of some other inferior metal. Yet they know they can not do so if I am still among you."

The sachem smiled. "That was my surmise as well. But we had little choice but to comply."

"Perhaps not," said Jacob. "But we may yet thwart their scheme." He went over to pick up a brass kettle, and brought it to the sachem. Taking his tomahawk, he ran the edge across it. "Do you see how deep a gouge my blade has made?"

The sachem nodded.

Jacob took up Hannah, and ran the blade over her pivot. He showed the sachem the pivot had hardly been scratched.

"I pressed equally hard against both the kettle and the pivot. Do you understand?"

The sachem's eyes gleamed, and he nodded. "We shall test the pivots the English supply us."

There seemed to be nothing else to say or do. Jacob took up his pack, nodded to the sachem, and opened the door.

The Englishman and Cicaho were awaiting him. "Are you ready to go?" he was asked.

He did not answer, but led the way to the village gate.

13 Terms of Exile

January, 1774

At the edge of the Hodenosaunee lands, the English officer produced a document from his pocket, and proceeded to read it in English.

"'I, Techusin, also known as Jacob Schram, do hereby acknowledge and agree that I am forever forbidden from returning to Hodenosaunee lands or to any territory east of Fort Pitt, or north of Fort Detroit. I am furthermore forbidden from any commerce, communication, or other intercourse with any inhabitant of said territories. I understand and agree that any infractions of these terms shall be considered insurrection against the crown which is a capital crime and shall be punished accordingly.' "

He handed the manuscript to Jacob, and withdrew a small vial of ink and a quill from a pocket. "Would you sign it please?" he asked, again in English.

Jacob stared at him in surprise. Even in the midst of the wilderness, the English were consummate bureaucrats. But what was shocking as well as surprising, was that the officer knew his white name. How could that be?

"How do you know I am Jacob Schram?"

The corner of the officer's lip twitched. "Do you deny you are?"

"No. But how did you know I was?"

The twitch became a cold smile. "How do you imagine a few thousands of English officers maintain order over millions of miles with hundreds of thousands of inhabitants both civilized and heathen?" He answered his own question. "With an exceedingly good system of information. You would do well to learn from this example; we have eyes and ears everywhere."

If he knows I am Jacob Schram, does he also know I am wanted for murder in the Pennsylvania Colony? He glanced at Cicaho. *Yet he cannot detain me while Cicaho remains; the Hodenosaunee were promised I would be set at liberty. Shall he try to arrest me when Cicaho has left?*

He eyed the officer. *I think he does not know of the murder charge. He does not seem treacherous. But he could be a good actor. How can I be sure?*

He pursed his lips. He decided he would demand the officer remain with Cicaho for half a day after he had been released. He knew Cicaho would not mind, and, if the Englishman truly intended to set him at his liberty, should not either.

But what is this about being forbidden to go east or north? I remember nothing of that.

If he could not go east of Fort Pitt, he could never return to Hannah and Mateo.

"Did the sachems of the Seneca agree I could not go east or north?" he asked Cicaho in Hodenosaunee.

He shook his head. "They did not agree to those restrictions."

"Then neither shall I." Jacob looked at the English officer. "You shall cross them out, if you please, and note that they are null and void."

The officer frowned and said, "These are the terms to which you must agree. If you fail to do so, you shall not be set at your liberty."

"Speak in Hodenosaunee," Jacob demanded, "so Cicaho can understand what is said."

The officer scowled at him, but translated what he had said.

"Then you shall have broken your agreement with the Seneca Sachems, and I shall return to them and inform them of your lies," said Cicaho coldly. He added weight to his words by placing his hand upon his tomahawk.

"Now did I say I would not abide by our agreement?" asked the officer nervously. "I shall certainly abide by it."

"Restricting me from going east or north were not parts of the agreement," said Jacob, "and they shall not be added now."

"I do not have the authority to change the document."

"The document as it is changes the agreement with the sachems. You do not have the authority to do that."

The officer stood and stared at Jacob and Cicaho for a long moment.

He did not expect any opposition. He is a man used to telling men like me what he demands and having them obey.

The man switched back to English. "Jacob, you are an intelligent man. You surely must know that, for his own reasons, General Hamilton in Fort Detroit refuses to allow you to cross those boundaries. I shall cross out the restrictions on this document if you demand, but you can be sure that if the general finds you north or east of those forts, and he shall, another pretext shall be found to arrest you. He shall not allow you to cross them; what is written upon this document shall not matter."

"It shall matter," replied Jacob, "in that, should I decide to cross them, I shall not be violating my word. I shall not be honor bound to regard them."

The officer gave him his first real smile. "As you wish." He opened the vial of ink, dipped the quill, and crossed out the offensive script. At the bottom he added, "The restrictions regarding passing the forts were not negotiated or agreed to and are null and void."

He looked up at Jacob. "Is that sufficient?"

Jacob nodded.

"Then will you sign it?"

Again Jacob nodded. He could tell Cicaho was getting anxious. He did not like that so much was transpiring in English and so was unintelligible to him. He smiled at him, said in Hodenosaunee, "It is well, my friend," and signed the document.

The officer carefully blew upon it and, taking a bit of cloth from his pocket, blotted it. "Thank you." He regarded Jacob shrewdly. "I trust you are wise enough to remain within the boundaries specified anyway. If you do not, you shall be pursued and it shall likely be I who am sent. I would prefer not to be faced with that task."

Jacob considered him gravely, and then grinned. "T'would be an interesting contest though, would it not?"

The Englishman laughed. "That it would." He grew serious. "I like you Jacob, or Techusin, if you prefer. But you must know that I shall do my duty, and if I am forced to pursue you, it can end in only three ways: I kill you, you kill me, or you are arrested and executed."

"Or you lose my trail, and I escape."

"I told you I have access to an exceedingly good network of information. Do not underestimate it." He paused pointedly. "I would hate to have to destroy you."

Jacob looked back into his eyes equally seriously. "No more would I enjoy having you as an enemy. But I cannot, and shall not, promise to remain within the boundaries. The best I can give you is that I have no intention at this time to cross them. But should my intentions change . . ."

"You shall at least know what the consequences would be."

"Aye." Jacob considered the officer. "You can be sure I shall only cross the boundaries after the most careful consideration."

The officer nodded. "I guess I shall have to be content with that."

"Am I free to go?" When the officer nodded, Jacob asked, "May I ask your name?"

The officer grinned, and held out his hand. "I'm sorry. I should have introduced myself when first we met. I am Lieutenant James Robinson."

Jacob shook his hand, and nodded. "Lieutenant Robinson, I cannot say it has been a pleasure, but I can say you have been courteous and a gentleman. I hope when next we meet it shall be under more mutually auspicious conditions."

He considered making the demand the officer remain with Cicaho for a half day but decided against it. He did not believe the lieutenant duplicitous enough to claim to release him only to then pursue and arrest him.

He turned to Cicaho. There was a great deal he wished he could tell the man, but was sure he already knew his feelings, so he contented himself with thanking him for accompanying him, and for being his friend. Then he turned upon his heel and left them.

14   Rogue Injin

November, 1774

As Jacob came in sight of the settlement nestled along the Kalcaska River his heart sank at the sight and smell. It was an obscene scar in the pristine forest. He dreaded spending the next four or five months in it.

The stench and ugliness however were not what caused Jacob to hesitate to commit himself to winter in the settlement; it was the attitude of many of its inhabitants. For, although Jacob's arrival the prior winter had been rather fortuitous for the settlers; he doubted they would have survived their first winter in the forest without his aid, they despised him as being too 'Indian.' His presence among them was tolerated but not welcomed. Yet he had found this to be the only white settlement within several hundred miles.

When the English officer had set him at his liberty at the edge of Hodenosaunee lands and had added the restrictions that Jacob was never to pass north of Fort Detroit nor east of Fort Pitt, Jacob had not known the territory open to him was nearly devoid of human inhabitants. Thus far he had discovered only seven tiny white settlements, three of which no longer existed. There were no permanent Indian settlements, only temporary hunting camps.

The territory was a vast buffer zone between the Iroquois Confederation on the north and powerful tribes to the south and west each of which claimed portions of it as private hunting grounds but none inhabited. He was forbidden to return to the Iroquois, and the tribes to the south and west would kill him on sight as an Iroquois which left his only source of companionship the few white settlers he found.

At first Jacob had been almost glad it was deserted; he was well able to live alone in the wilderness and feared allowing anyone to become too precious to him. *If I love no one, I need not fear losing them.* But time and again his longing for fellowship had driven him back to the settlement on the Kalkaska River despite their lack of welcome.

But now that he was here, he was loath to commit himself.

He was trying to force himself to enter the settlement when he heard a turkey gobble. It sounded like a big tom, not far away. He grinned to himself; bringing in a plump tom would no doubt enhance his welcome and be a good excuse to delay his entry. He turned and plunged back into the forests.

It was not long before he spotted a buck slipping away before him; he must have come too close to where it had been bedded.

Yeh need not fear, brother. I'm not on yer trail this time.

He noticed a thicket just ahead of the buck.

Aye. I see where yer headed. Good idea, yeh'd be hard to follow in there and yeh'll no doubt find a soft place to nest.

But to his surprise, the buck snorted and veered away from the thicket.

Jacob stopped and sank silently to his haunches.

Now why did he do that? What is in that thicket that spooked him? A hunter mayhap?

He did not think it could be. If he were in the midst of the forest he could believe it might be an Indian hunter, but he knew no Indian would come this close to a settlement and he did not believe any of the white settlers could sit quietly enough that he would not have heard him.

Hear him? Jacob chuckled to himself quietly. *More likely I'd smell him before I'd hear him.*

Jacob had retained the habit, acquired from the Iroquois, of bathing every morning while most of the settlers bathed twice a year, once in the spring when they changed from winter to summer garb and again in the fall when they changed back to their winter garb.

Beside, like as not the fool would be puffin' on one o' his pipes.

It could be a bear. But he discarded that idea as well. If it was earlier or later in the year, he could believe a bear was sleeping there, but not in the fall; this was when bears were all loading themselves up with a layer of fat; they didn't have time for sleep while the sun shone.

Jacob slowly crept around the thicket. He very soon found evidence of a man having gone into the thicket, clearly one of the settlers. He continued to circle the thicket and came upon the marks of someone who had come out of the thicket and proceeded east; this man was clearly an Indian. He felt the hair on the back of his neck stand up.

Now what was an Indian doing this close to the settlement?

Clearly nothing good. He proceeded with much greater caution, and soon came upon where the Indian had entered the thicket. But though he continued until he had completed the circuit back to where he had begun, Jacob found no evidence that the settler had come out.

With dread he slipped into the thicket himself. He soon found what he expected, a scalped corpse.

He was sitting on his haunches considering what he should best do, inform the settlement, or chase the Indian before he got too far away, when he heard the unmistakable sound of a settler approaching.

Jamie's breeches, can't they walk through the forest quieter than that? Tis a wonder they manage to kill any game.

He slipped out of the copse to where he could see him.

It was Mr. Sullivan, the leader of the settlement.

For a moment Jacob considered not revealing himself. *It is not really my affair. What'll I do if the settlers blame me for the murder? How do I know they won't? Most of them despise me enough to believe I'd kill and scalp someone.*

But his conscience would not allow him to fail to inform Mr. Sullivan.

I doubt they know the man is even missing, let alone dead; he hasn't been dead more than a few hours. They'd likely not find him until he started to stink, mayhap not even then. Besides, alerting them may save some of their lives; if that Indian killed once, he'll likely try again.

He stepped into Mr. Sullivan's path and called to him quietly.

The man jumped and exclaimed loudly, "Tarnation, Jacob, don't be jumping out at a man like that. Yeh dang near give me the fantogs."

"Hush," Jacob hissed.

Dang fool, tell the whole world we're here. Aint he got no sense a'tall?

He stepped quickly up to him and said quietly, "Yeh got a man dead yonder. Somewhere close is an Injun; lessen yeh want to join yer friend, yeh'd best be silent."

The man's eyes gaped. "A killer Injun? Where?"

"I aint sure. Somewhere to the east, I think." He pointed into the thicket. "Yer friend is in there. He aint pretty."

"Tarnation." The man looked at the thicket fearfully; he did not look eager to search it. He turned and grabbed Jacob's arm. "Good Lord, Jacob, what are we gonna do? If there's a killer Injun stalkin' us, how are we to procure our winter supply of meat? There aint none o' us up to facing such a savage." He looked at Jacob hopefully.

Jacob considered him coldly. He had intended to track the Indian down and deal with him, and he had planned to do it alone. He had no intention of allowing some settler to get him killed by some foolishness; he would be much safer on his own.

But watching Mr. Sullivan practically plead for him to deal with the Indian made him despise him. What kind of a man would beg another to do something he was afraid to attempt, particularly when it is none of the other man's affair?

"What do yeh say, Jacob, will yeh come to our aid? Will yeh rid the forest of this menace?"

Jacob did not bother to answer him, just nodded curtly, turned on his heel, and went to where he had seen the Indian's trail.

15   Mano e Mano

November, 1774

Some little distance ahead, Jacob again heard the tom. He stopped and thought.

Of course. He saw it now. *Why was that settler in the woods? For that matter, why was Mr. Sullivan? They were both chasing that tom, I bet.*

It's dang easy to imitate a tom turkey.

He grinned to himself. *At least this'll make things a bit easier for me.*

He abandoned the Indian's trail, and went north and then far to the east, and circled back toward the settlement. It wasn't long before he heard the tom. He listened carefully. He didn't blame the settlers for having been fooled; it sounded just like a tom all right; a big one. He moved very carefully closer. The gobble was coming from the midst of a small valley.

It wasn't right.

It would be exactly right for a tom, but not for an Indian in ambush. An Indian in the middle of the valley wouldn't see a hunter until he was almost upon him. That meant . . . Jacob scanned the surrounding hilltops. There were two Indians; one of them on a hilltop.

But which one? He knew better than to move until he knew. He spotted two eagles soaring in the sky. He watched them as they slowly worked their way across the valley, back and forth, slowly drifting north. He noticed they avoided the air directly above a small grove next to the stream which wound through the valley. That was where the 'tom' was. He kept watching.

There! One of the eagles had turned short of one of the hills. He watched to see if he would turn short on his next pass. He did. The eagle's mate was coming up to it. Would she turn short also? She did.

That was where his quarry was, on that hill top; he was sure of it. The question was how to get to it without being seen. He scanned the terrain surrounding the hilltop. The Indian had chosen his post well; there was no way to approach the hill without being seen. Jacob considered staying where he was until dark; the Indians had to camp sometime. But he discarded the idea. He knew the Indians could detect his presence the same way he had detected theirs; maybe already had.

He noticed the hill just this side of his quarry was taller than the Indian post and, if Jacob were to work his way carefully, he could gain its summit. From there he might be able to discover the Indian's precise location. He began his stalk.

* * * *

He felt exposed on the summit; from high ground he could see much further, but he knew he could also be seen from much further. He still could see nothing on the next hilltop. He chose a tree and climbed it. There was a break in the foliage which afforded him a grand view.

He sucked in his breath. There the Indian was; in a tree on the next hill. He scanned the ground between them. How could he get to him?

He couldn't.

It would be a very long shot, but this was as close as he was going to get.

He considered his options. Once he fired his rifle, everything would be changed; the Indians would know of his presence and location. He would become the prey. But he was quite certain there were only two of them; he wasn't too concerned. He would only have to make it to the edge of the settlement; they would not pursue him further.

He settled himself on the limb and licked his finger to wet Hannah's sight. It was best to act promptly; at any moment the Indian might discern his presence. He slowly extended Hannah until she was trained on the target. He exhaled slowly and held it. His finger slowly tightened. Hannah barked, and the Indian fell from the tree.

Jacob watched him fall but immediately turned to watch the copse of trees where he knew the 'tom' lurked. He saw no movement. He glanced back at the fallen Indian. No movement there either. It was hard to believe he was dead; more likely stunned by the fall. Jacob knew if that was the case, he would not remain stunned for long.

He glanced back at the copse. Did he dare risk going to finish off the first Indian? He knew it was very risky. But was it more risky than allowing the stunned Indian to recover? He decided it was not.

He climbed quickly but quietly from the tree, reloaded Hannah, and hurried to the next hill. He peered around a tree carefully at the fallen man. As he had guessed, he was not dead, but only gut shot; he was already regaining his senses. Jacob glanced again at the copse; no movement yet. Where was that other Indian? What was he doing?

He loosened his tomahawk, burst from his cover to bash the Indian's head in, and slid back to the brush. At least that was one less to worry about.

Where was that other Indian? There was still no sign of movement from the copse. Could it be the other Indian did not yet know of his presence? He would have heard only the one shot; perhaps he had not known his partner's exact location.

How best can I sneak up on the copse?

He decided his best approach would be the direct one. If the other Indian did not yet know of his presence, he would likely believe him to be his partner. He moved boldly but stealthily directly down the hill and to the copse. He circled it carefully, and then slipped in.

He spied the Indian; crouched behind a fallen tree. He leaned Hannah silently against a tree, took his tomahawk in hand,

and burst upon him. He yanked the Indian's head up by the hair and his tomahawk was already descending when he realized the face staring up at him was not that of a warrior, but of a woman, not much more than a girl.

He stopped his blow just inches from her face, but her hand slashed at his stomach with a sharpened bit of wood; he only just avoided it. He slammed her against the log and knocked the wood from her hand with his knee. But she fought like a wildcat; scratching, clawing, and yowling.

Durn girl, he thought grimly as he fought her*; doesn't she realize I could have killed her, still could kill her easily?* He didn't want to kill her. But he wasn't going to let her go either.

He finally subdued her by bulk of strength and weight and tied her hand and foot. He sat gasping for breath and surveyed her lying before him. *Why is she here? Is she the killer's cohort or his slave?* He had never heard of an Indian woman who went on the war path. He turned from her to retrieve his rifle.

What am I to do with her? I can't take her back to the settlement; they'd hang her for sure. He walked back to her, squatted down, and considered her. *Maybe I should let them hang her; she has lured at least one man to his death; likely more.* But he knew he wouldn't, couldn't. She was little more than a girl and besides, she was an Indian; she had only done what had been right for her to do.

"What is your name?" he asked in Huron. She did not reply. He repeated the question in Ojibwa. She remained silent, but he was sure she had understood. He grabbed a handful of her hair and forced her to look at him. "I asked you for your name."

She spat in his face. *The little vixen!* By Jamie, he liked this gal; she had some spunk. He laughed and wiped her spittle off in her hair. "If you won't tell me," he said, "I'll call you Bluh-luh-luh-lah" He could imitate a tom turkey too. Was that a smile he saw? If it was, it was a brief one. He grinned down at her. "So what's it to be, that or your real name?'

She met his gaze a moment and then looked away. "I am called, Wahanaosai," she finally answered. She had a distinct accent; one he had never heard.

"What people are you?"

She again considered him for a moment before answering, "Illinois"

He was surprised. He had heard of the Illinois, but had never before seen one. "Why are you so far east?"

She considered him, but refused to answer.

"My name is Techusin," he said.

Her eyes narrowed. "You lie. That is the name of a snake man, an Iroquois."

"I was Iroquois; a Seneca. They adopted me."

For the first time he saw fear in her eyes; but it was quickly quenched. "Then we are enemies."

"We need not be."

Her eyes narrowed again, and she stared at him coldly. "The Iroquois never make peace with an Indian not of the confederation; even the Illinois know this."

He stared into her eyes. "I said I was Iroquois. I did not say I am."

"Why are you not?"

"The English forced them to send me away."

"Pah," she spat, "The English; how I hate them."

Jacob sat back in surprise. "You hate the English? But are you not serving them?"

"No."

"Why then do you kill the settlers?"

She stared at him calculatingly for several moments and then answered, "For their scalps. The English commander, Hamilton, in Detroit will pay much for them."

"Is that not serving the English?"

"I don't serve them."

Jacob was amused by the scowl upon her face. It seemed to him that she had been serving them. But he was surprised she had so freely told him their motives. It was his turn to be suspicious. "Why have you told me this?"

She stared at the ground and said, "Because it does not matter if I tell you; you shall soon be dead." She glanced up at him and cocked her head to one side. "You should be dead already. How did you get to me alive?"

He considered her and answered calmly, "I am alive because I first killed a man; there." He pointed at the hill and watched her reaction.

Her eyes widened. "You killed him?" She looked at him with respect. "Many have tried; all have failed."

"Who have tried," Jacob asked. "Why have they tried?"

Her stoic face faltered and she stared at the ground. He saw several tears etch their course down her cheeks; for the first time he realized how dirty they were. "My two brothers tried," she whispered, "and many others." She looked up at him with a glare. "He was a renegade; no tribe would abide him. He stole me from my people, my family, and my home. He killed my brothers when they came for me. He killed many, many men." She looked at him pleadingly. "He forced me to lure men to me; I did not wish to. He would have killed me if I had not."

Jacob considered her story; dare he believe her? He decided he did, but that did not mean he trusted her. What was he to do with her?

He stood. The first thing to do, he decided, was to find their camp. That would tell him a great deal concerning them. Then he would know better whether to trust her. "Where is your camp?"

She pointed her chin to the west, beyond the settlement. "It is there; long walk. You would not find it, but I shall show you."

He took his knife and cut her bonds. "I would find it," he said. "But you shall show me."

"First show me . . . him," she pled.

He was pleased she disdained to use his name. Refusal to use a dead man's name deprived him of memory; erased him from existence. It validated her story; no Indian would deprive any but their greatest enemy of memory. He led her to the corpse.

She stood staring at it for several long moments. "My brothers are avenged," she finally said, "Let us go," and, without another glance, began to walk north.

"Wait," Jacob called, and he stripped the man of his weapons, powder horn, and shot bag before following her.

The campsite was as he had expected and verified her claims. It was plain she had slept bound to a log; her captor had not even provided her with a blanket. There were ample supplies of food and gun powder; and twenty scalps; most of them white, but a few Indian. He gathered everything of any value into a pack and handed it to her.

"What are you going to do with me?" she asked.

"What do you want me to do with you?"

She shrugged.

"I thought you would want me to take you back to your people."

Her eyes narrowed. "Why would you do that?"

He looked at her levelly. "Because I was taken from my people. I wish someone could take me back, but I know it shall never be."

"Why do you not take yourself?"

He shook his head. She did not understand. She did not know what an ocean was. How could he explain it to her? He did not want to try. "It shall never be," he simply repeated. "But I shall return you." He grinned at her. "I have never been to the land of the Illinois."

He did not tell her, but he hoped she would prove the key he needed to escape the void the English had exiled him in. Surely being accompanied by an Illinois woman would grant him passage through the lands of the tribes to the west. Somewhere in the west, perhaps with the Illinois themselves, he would find a tribe which would not recognize him as an Iroquois or care. He did not wish to remain alone.

She stared at him and finally asked, "Why must I carry the pack?" Her chin rose. "I shall not be your servant."

"You shall carry the pack," he said, "because it is your pack."

"My pack?"

He shrugged. "I don't want it, and I expect you deserve it if any one does."

She stared at him in pleased amazement, but then dropped the pack and fished out the scalps. "I don't want these."

"Put them back," he ordered her. "Didn't you say the commander at Detroit would pay for them?" He stuffed them back into the pack and tied it shut. "We shall go to Detroit first and collect our reward."

She glared at him in dismay. "I shall not serve the English," she said.

"Nor shall I," he said. "The English were already served by these men's deaths. We cannot change that, but we can require of the English the promised bounty." He threw the pack into her arms. "We shall go to the settlement for supplies I shall require of them. Then we shall visit Detroit and collect our bounty. Then I shall return you to your Illinois." He turned to go.

She followed him. "But," she said, "I cannot go into the settlement. They shall kill me."

"Not if you are with me," he assured her. "I shall tell them you are my squaw."

She jumped in front of him with her eyes blazing. "I am not your squaw!"

He laughed, and calmly stepped around her. "They shall not know that."

She followed him, but repeated, "I am not your squaw."

16   Fort Detroit

January, 1775

Jacob and Wahanaosai rounded a bend in the river, and Fort Detroit was finally visible in the distance. Jacob stood for a moment and stared at it with mixed emotions.

On the one hand, it was a very welcome sight. It signaled the end of one leg of their long trek and promised relief from the cold northern winds which had plagued them for the past week. Walking upon the frozen river made for easy travel, level and without obstructions, but it also exposed them to the full brunt of the elements. Despite Jacob's dislike of cities, the thought of walls between him and the January winds was pleasant.

Yet the very fact that it signaled the end of one leg of their trek filled Jacob with remorse. As he and Wahanaosai had traveled ever west, the conviction had grown upon him that he was making a mistake. Every day was adding weary miles between himself and where he truly wished to be: with Hannah and Mateo. And Detroit stood as a brutal reminder of why he could not go to them, the power of the English, and the edict which restrained him.

He sighed deeply, and resumed his march to the citadel.
* * * *
Later, as he strode through the narrow alleys of the sprawling buildings surrounding Fort Detroit, he struggled to

restrain his revulsion. When he and Wahanaosai had first spotted the fort, it had seemed terrible, forbidding, but beautiful. He had often heard Detroit described as the premier fort of the English; those English officers he had encountered from Detroit boasted it had never been taken by an enemy. Now that Jacob had seen it, he could understand why; the fort was formidably built and even better positioned, sitting athwart and controlling the crossroads of the west.

The fort itself, the crew quarters, and the official buildings associated with it were just as impressive as his first sight had promised. But behind them, crowded against the fort by the lowlands which encroached upon it, were the dwellings of those wretches which always gathered at, and did the real work of, any great edifice. It was among them Jacob was seeking lodging; he had been informed General Hamilton was away and not expected back for a week, and no bounties were going to be paid until his return. But he had quickly discovered exorbitant fees were demanded for room and board in the more reputable habitations, and thus was seeking lodging among the more decrepit, far from the fort, and hard against the swamp.

The stench was quite offensive, but from one hovel he detected a pleasant aroma of cooking. He looked at Wahanaosai, she shrugged, and he knocked upon its door. It was answered by a hugely pregnant Indian woman with a small child clinging to her skirt.

"Forgive my intrusion," he said, "but my companion," he indicated Wahanaosai, "and I are looking for a place to lodge for a few days. Would you perchance have room for us? We would be content with anything you may have to offer, and shall pay a shilling per day."

Jacob had thought a shilling so deep within the wilderness would be considered a great deal of money, but had found it was not regarded as such near Detroit.

The woman looked at him suspiciously, and then stared at the floor. "I . . . I have little to feed you." She glared at him. "I have trouble enough feeding myself and my child."

Jacob produced the two rabbits he had hanging from his belt, and offered them. "If you provide us with lodging, we shall not only feed ourselves, but share our meat with you."

The woman's eyes glowed, and she nodded.

He soon found the cabin had a liberal loft which was offered Wahanaosai and him, but he saw only the one cot on the lower floor.

"Does the child sleep in the loft?" he presumed to ask the woman.

She was bent over the table dressing the rabbits, but shook her head. "She sleeps with me."

"With your man?" demanded Wahanaosai.

The woman shook her head.

"You have no man," Wahanaosai stated, ignoring Jacob's sharp glance.

Has the woman no tack or compassion?

"I used to," the poor woman said sadly. "I was married to a lieutenant of the fort. When he was here, I did not live in this hut." She looked up, and her chin rose. "No. I once lived in one of the finest houses right next to the fort's gate. Life was good then." Her head dropped again to her task, and she muttered, "But now he is gone."

"Is he dead?" Jacob asked sympathetically.

She shook her head. "No, just gone. He was transferred to Fort Michilimackinac and could not take us with him."

He left you and his child behind? In squalor and poverty? Jacob could not imagine a man doing such a thing.

But Wahanaosai had caught his eye and scowled. "Many white men leave their Indian wives," she said to him disdainfully. Her chin rose. "I would never marry a white man."

Jacob glared at her, and glanced at the woman. He was sure she had heard. *It may be true she did not make a good choice in her marriage, but it is cruel to abuse her for it now.*

He realized the tiny child was staring up at him. Her mother had noticed it also.

"You remind her of her father," she said apologetically. "She misses him."

I hope I am nothing like her father.

But he went to his pack lying in the corner, fished out a small rock of sugar he had obtained at the fort earlier, knelt, and offered it to the girl.

She came to him timidly, took the rock, popped it into her mouth, and smiled.

She is an attractive little waif when she smiles. It was clear she was half white. "What is her name?"

Her mother smiled at them. "Sybil."

Sybil? What a horrid name for such a charming child. He was sure her father must have named her that; no Indian would choose such a name. His loathing of the man grew.

"How old is she?" he heard Wahanaosai ask.

So she can be civil and polite. Jacob had begun to doubt it.

"She is two." It was clear the mother was proud of her child, and enjoyed talking about her.

"What is your name?" Jacob asked.

"Yimsotha."

"Yimsotha. That sounds like . . . Miami? Ojibwa?"

"Ojibwa," she confirmed.

"If you do not mind my asking, could you not return to them?"

Her eyes dropped. "No. That can never be."

Jacob felt sorry for her. *She is not my concern,* he reminded himself. *I cannot rescue everyone I meet that needs help.* But as he looked around the cabin, he saw it was in very poor repair. *I can at least spend my days awaiting the general's return improving it.*

17   Shoshanna

January, 1775

Jacob whistled cheerfully as he walked down the dirty snowy alley leading to the cabin. He had had a prosperous morning. Not only had he snared three rabbits and a coon, he had succeeded in trading one rabbit for several onions and another for some potatoes. He had the makings of a first rate meal. In addition, he had chopped some wood for a man, and received several dozen cedar shingles in return. By night, if all went well, he expected to have the leak in the roof fixed.

But some distance from the cabin, he heard Sybil wailing. He burst in to find Yinsotha panting in her bed with Wahanaosai sitting beside her holding her hand. Jacob looked from them to Sybil, crouched in a corner sobbing.

"It is her time," Wahanaosai said simply. "She says there is a woman who lives in the back of the miller's who served as her midwife when Sybil was born. Fetch her."

Jacob dropped the food and shingles in a corner and ran to the miller. When he arrived, the miller was busy with several customers, but Jacob interrupted him. "Is there a midwife here?"

The miller turned and considered him calmly. "Aye," he said slowly and scratched his neck. "Yeh'll be wanting me mother-in-law. Molly," he called to a young girl. "Fetch yer granny. Tell her her services be needed." The girl ran.

The miller nodded at Jacob. "Yeh'll be the young buck who moved in with that Injin gal, Yinsotha." When Jacob nodded, he said, "The ald woman's been expecting a call from her." He looked Jacob up and down and then grinned. "I'm right glad Yinsotha found herself a man to take the lieutenant's place. Tis a good woman there; she didn't deserve to be treated so."

"But I'm not her . . .," Jacob started to protest, but the miller had already turned back to his customers and Molly had returned with a wizened old woman who must be the midwife, so Jacob left the miller to his illusions, took the old woman's arm, and tried to hurry her along to Yimsotha's.

But the woman refused to be hurried. She laughed at Jacob. "This yer first time?" When Jacob admitted it was, she patted his arm and said, "Take it from someone who's seen a good many, we've plenty of time. How long has it been since she started?"

"I do not know," Jacob said, "When I returned she was in the midst of them. She did not say for how long, only sent me after you."

"Well in that case . . ." The old woman picked up her pace remarkably.

They were soon at the cabin, and the woman took charge, issuing orders with a calm efficiency. The change in the atmosphere was immediate. Even Sybil stopped sobbing, and merely sat watching with an occasional whimper.

"She is far too young to witness such a thing," proclaimed the midwife, "but now that she knows her mother is in pain, we cannot send her away. You, boy." She pointed at Jacob. "Your task shall be to distract her."

Me? What do I know of comforting a tiny girl? And she hardly knows me; she may be afraid of me.

But he went to her, sat beside her, and lifted her into his lap. To his surprise, she did not resist. *She is not much younger than Ailantha had been when first I met her.* Jacob missed having Ailantha snuggle in his lap and reflexively wrapped his arms about her and held her close. "Would you like me to tell you a story?"

The little girl shook her head; she seemed content to merely snuggle. There was little noise from the bed, only an occasional huffing or quiet moan, interspersed with murmured commands from the midwife, but Jacob noticed that whenever there was a noise, Sybil would tense and tremble. He had to distract her, or at least drown out the noise.

Since she did not want to hear a story, he decided to hum a few tunes. To his joy, she seemed to like that; she smiled up at him, and snuggled tighter against his breast; she seemed to like feeling the vibrations of his voice. After a while she grew limp, and he realized she had fallen asleep.

He gently removed the hair from her face, and sat watching her sleep. He had almost forgotten how much he enjoyed holding a child. He felt himself begin to nod.

They were both shocked awake by a shriek from the bed followed by several guttural moans. Almost immediately thereafter came a thin but lusty wail.

"It's a fine baby girl," the midwife announced in Algonquin.

Jacob grinned down into the fearful eyes of Sybil. "You have a baby sister. Do you want to see her?" He began to rise with her, but the midwife commanded, "No. Yeh stay where yeh be. She has yet to deliver the afterbirth, and that aint a fit sight for a child. The gal here," she indicated Wahanaosai, "shall bring her to yeh."

Shortly the tiny babe was presented to them, washed and wrapped in a small blanket. Jacob thought she was perhaps the single most ugly creature he had ever seen, red, misshapen, and blotchy, but Sybil was enchanted, cooing and touching the baby tentatively.

The delightful moment was spoiled however, by the midwife's anxious call. "We have trouble. Jacob, she's asking for yeh."

Jacob handed the babe back to Wahanaosai, and hurried to the bedside. "What is wrong?"

"She is bleeding." The midwife looked at him with weary sad eyes, and shook her head. "I've seen it before. There is naught I can do." She shrugged resignedly. "It may stop. It may not."

Jacob felt his hand grasped by Yinsotha. He looked down to see her eyes pleading with him. She was trying to speak but could not muster the breath. He leaned down to her.

"Jacob," she whispered desperately, "my babies." She tried to say more, but her strength failed her.

"I will care for them," he swore. "Before God I will."

She smiled at him, and then slowly her eyes lost their luster and became fixed.

"She is gone, poor gal," announced the midwife. She patted Jacob on the shoulder. "Tis sorry I am." She turned to go.

Jacob tore himself away from sight of the dead mother, and called, "Wait." He went to the game in the corner. "I haven't much money, but if yeh'd accept a rabbit or coon for your trouble, I'd be obliged."

"That'd suit me just fine," the old woman said with a grin. "I'm right partial ta coon, that I am. Taint often I get one." She took it from his hand, and nodded. "Thank'e" Then she was gone.

Jacob stood in shock for several moments, unwilling to return to the horror behind him until he became aware that Sybil was again sobbing. He went to her, and took her in his arms.

How do you explain to such a wee lass that her mother has just died?

He looked to Wahanaosai. "What shall we do? What is to become of her?"

"Kill her, as I have killed her sister."

Jacob looked in horror to find the tiny babe was on the floor dead.

"It is the only thing to do," said Wahanaosai with cold logic. "She shall die anyway."

Jacob clutched the girl to his breast protectively. "No, she shall not. Did you not hear me swear to her mother I would care for her, for both of them? I shall take her as my daughter."

Wahanaosai's chin rose. "I shall not travel to the Illinois with her. She would slow us down. And I cannot return to my people with a half breed child and a white man! Everyone would believe I am your squaw and the brat is ours. I shall not do it."

Jacob stood and stared coldly down upon her. Her selfish rejection of Sybil repulsed him even more than her murder of the baby had. He loathed her and could not abide remaining with her another moment let alone for the weeks it would require to escort her to the Illinois.

"You are right, you shall not. You shall go alone. I will take the girl and return to the east."

Wahanaosai gaped, and then became angry. "You will abandon me? You promised you would return me to my people." Her voice became desperate. "I cannot travel alone through the forest. What is to become of me?"

"Who needs me more?" Jacob asked coldly. "You or her? You made your choice to go on alone when you refused to allow her to accompany us. I had already told you I had taken her as my daughter."

He set Sybil down carefully, brought his pack to her, and opened it.

"Sybil, child," he said, and then paused, considering his words. *How can I explain to her she must come with me?* He did not wish to lie, yet neither did he think it best to tell her her mother was dead and she would never again see her.

He squatted before her. "Your mother asked me to take you with me to another place. Your mother must remain here for a while. Can you be a very brave little girl and gather up whatever you want to take with you?"

She stared at him soberly for several moments, but then nodded and brought him her few possessions. While she did so, he removed the bracelets from her mother's wrists, and stored them safely away. *Someday*, he thought, *the child shall want something of her mother's, she deserves to have them.*

As he tied his pack shut, he saw Sybil was staring up at her mother's bed.

"You want to say goodbye." She nodded, and he lifted her up to sit beside her mother. He wished he had thought to close her eyes.

But the child merely stroked her mother's arm and then laid her head upon her breast. After a few moments she looked up at him, and asked, "Did Jesus take my mommy away?"

So she knows her mother is dead. And she has been raised a Christian.

"Yes," Jacob said, "He did."

Her face crumpled, she stood, and held out her arms to him. He took her up, and she buried her face in his shoulder and sobbed.

Jacob managed to shrug his arms through the loops of rope supporting his pack. Wahanaosai had watched all of their actions angrily, but had not said a word.

"The scalps are in your pack," he said. "Get whatever bounty you may and either be on your way, or remain and become someone's squaw. I do not care which."

He set the child down, gently placed her dead sister in her mother's arms, and closed both of their eyes. He then wrapped the child snuggly in a blanket, and picked up his rifle. "Shoshanna and I are leaving."

"Shoshanna?"

"That is her name now." Jacob had named her after his favorite aunt. He had always liked that name. He turned his back upon Wahanaosai and left the house of horror.

It bothered him a bit to leave the two corpses unattended, but he reminded himself his concern must be the living not the dead. *Yinsotha is beyond caring what I do and, were I to remain, even for a few hours, the ever practical Wahanaosai would doubtless kill Shoshanna in the hope I would then agree to continue my trek to the Illinois.*

As Detroit disappeared around a bend in the river, the child's sobs faded into whimpers. He wished he could find a way to comfort her, but how do you ease the pain of a child who has lost her mother? He could not.

But, as he roasted a muskrat over the fire he had built after making camp that evening, the child crawled into his lap, and clung to him. *Somehow she knows I mean her well.*

He held and rocked her gently.

18   Take Me Home

February, 1777

Jacob slipped quietly up to the cabin as was his habit, knowing it was a foolish remnant of a game. When he had first gotten his dog, Takawni, he had been a tiny pup. Then it had been a game to try to sneak up on the cabin without the dog detecting his approach. But it had been many months since he had last succeeded in doing so. Still Jacob enjoyed trying.

Besides, even if the dog no doubt had detected him, he might yet surprise Shoshanna. In the two years since he had adopted her, the girl had blossomed into a bewitching waif.

He listened carefully; there was no sound from within. He grinned and opened the door, and Shoshanna leaped up from where she had been sitting with her dog and into his arms.

"Look Papa, look what I taught Takawni." She slipped from his arms, ran to the dog, and whispered to him. Instantly the dog transformed himself into a snarling stalking beast with the hair of his back bristling with threat. A vicious low growl issued from between savage fangs.

Jacob knew he would never harm him, but he still felt his heart skip a beat. Had it been any other dog, he would not have remained in the cabin with him. Even as it was, he was careful in his movements. "That is very good," he said to Shoshanna.

She laughed, and whispered again to the dog, which immediately dropped to the floor, and became again the happy gentle giant Jacob knew him to be.

Jacob went over and scratched the dog behind his ear. "Good boy, Takawni." He knew if a stranger had presumed to enter the cabin the performance would have been real. This dog was why he could leave his daughter alone for the many hours he needed to walk his trap line; with him by her side, he knew she had nothing to fear.

Still, it bothered him to leave her as he did. He knew the hours alone were often dreary. As excellent as he was, Takawni could not replace human companionship.

He sighed. He and the girl lived alone, in the midst of the forest. It was a life to which he had become accustomed, even enjoyed, but he was becoming increasingly aware it was a life unfair to the vivacious girl. She had been used to being surrounded by people, to the crowded conditions around Fort Detroit. She, unlike he, enjoyed such crowds.

I cannot continue to raise her as I am, isolated and alone. She needs friends and she needs to be around women. But what could he do, where could he go?

He went to the cauldron hanging over the fire, and checked the stew he had made that morning. *A few biscuits would go good with that.*

He went to his bag of flour, and soon had a batch baking in the oven he had fashioned in the wall of the fireplace. He had discovered he liked baking breads; perhaps there was more of his father in him than he had realized as a boy. He chuckled to himself. He knew the truer reason he liked to bake was that he liked to eat breads. He tried to forget how many furs he had been forced to trade for that bag of flour.

As the biscuits baked, he watched Shoshanna playing contentedly beside him. Perhaps he ought to return her to Detroit. Surely somewhere in that mass of humanity someone could be found who would take her.

No, he revolted, *not take her.* She had become very dear to him; he would never be able to give her up.

But would there not be some way to support himself and her at Detroit. He was forbidden from passing the fort, but nothing forbade him from abiding there. But he quickly discarded the idea; the thought filled him with revulsion. He knew he could not long endure such a life.

If only there were a settlement somewhere which would accept them. The thought of establishing himself in a small intimate society was appealing. But he knew that hope was forlorn. The prejudice of the white settlers against the Indians was too universal and pronounced. A half breed child would never be accepted by them, and he would not subject her to such an environment.

If only the white settlers were as accepting as the Frenchies. Jacob did not like Frenchies, but he had heard they had many half breeds living among them; many were themselves half breeds. For Shoshanna's sake he would have been willing to overcome his revulsion, and abide with them. But, of course the Frenchie settlements were either north of Fort Detroit, or far to the west.

So where can I go? He did not know.

So, thrusting his worries aside, he ladled the stew into bowls, set the hot biscuits on the table, and called his daughter to eat. But, although the girl ate with gusto, and told him the meal was delicious, Jacob was unable to eat. He felt himself descending into a rare depression.

God of heaven and earth, what am I to do? Tell me what You would have me do, and I shall do it. But I need you to show me the way.

He finally gave up eating, and pushed his bowl away.

Shoshanna had finished her meal, and came, crawled up into his lap, and snuggled into his arms. He could see she could tell he was disheartened. But then she looked up at him, smiled, and asked, "Would you tell me a story, Papa?"

Jacob smiled back at her, his spirit already rebounding. *Sweet little imp, she seems always to discern how to cheer me.* Often it was by requesting a story; she knew he enjoyed telling them almost as much as she enjoyed hearing them.

"What kind of story would you like to hear?"

She thought for a moment, and then demanded, "Tell me a story about Uncle Mateo." She grinned, and laid her head against his breast expectantly. "They are always so funny."

"A story of Uncle Mateo, eh?" He had told her many stories of his brother's exploits, those of Hannah as well. He enjoyed remembering them. "Now what could I tell you that I haven't already told you?" He thought for a moment. "Ah, yes, I remember one." He laughed at the memory. "You shall like this one."

"You remember we used to go to see the old Indian, Woosamequin, every Sunday, do you not?"

She nodded.

"Well, every other Sunday, the Gerbers, who were Amish, would go to their meetings; the Amish met for the entire day with the others from their church. On those Sundays, so that the Gerbers would not have to hurry home, Mateo and I would return early, and do the evening chores by ourselves. Then, if it was hot, we would take a swim in the creek, and of course we swam naked. As long as we were sure to get out before the sun began to set, and the Gerbers returned, we knew we were safe, for the farm was nigh a mile from the nearest neighbor. Every other Sunday though was the only time it was safe to go swimming, for the rest of the time, Mrs. Gerber and their girls were always home, and the creek could be seen from the house."

He paused until the girl looked up at him. "But one day when I came home from the smithy, Mateo was nowhere to be found, the Gerbers were quite worried. It seems a friend of theirs had taken ill, and so Mr. Gerber had taken his wife and daughters to visit him, leaving Mateo to hoe the corn field. When they had returned, the field was hoed, and the evening chores had been done, but Mateo was missing. I guessed immediately that he had taken the opportunity to get a swim, but I could not imagine why he had not slipped out of the creek, and quickly dressed when he heard them returning.

"It worried me a little, but I told the family I thought I might find him by the creek, and would check.

"'Oh, we already checked by the creek,' the young girls chorused, 'He was not there.'

"'I'll check again,' I said, 'just to be sure,'" and Jacob laughed.

"Was he there?" asked Shoshanna.

"Oh, yes. And I soon heard him calling me quietly from a group of cattails. When I asked him why he had not gotten out and dressed, he replied he had not been able to for he had not expected the Gerbers to return so soon. He had been very hot after hoeing the corn field, and the barn was hot too, so he had stripped off his clothes, and done the chores naked, and then ran down for a swim. His clothes were still in the barn. He had been afraid to try to run all the way to the barn when he heard them returning, and then it had been too late."

Shoshanna giggled. "What did he do?"

"Well, of course, I went and got his clothes. But he had to don them in the center of the cattails even though it meant getting his pants wet. He could not come ashore without being seen. I asked him what he had done when the girls had come looking for him, and he said he had just hunkered down and kept quiet hoping they would not notice him.

"I told him he should have asked them to get his clothes. But for some reason, your Uncle Mateo did not think that was funny."

"That was a good story," Shoshanna said. But then she looked up at him seriously, and said, "I wish I could see him sometime. Hannah too. You have told me so many stories about them, but you have never taken me to see them. Why have you not?"

'It is a long story, my liebkin. I wish you could meet them, but I fear it shall never be." He stood with her in his arms, and carried her to her bed. "It is time for you to go to sleep while I clean up from our meal."

She stripped off her outer garments, and he knelt with her as she said her evening prayers as he had taught her. Then he tucked her in, and kissed her good night. It was one of his joys, to kiss her good night each evening.

As he washed their bowls, and fed Takawni, he wondered how his brother and Hannah were doing. It had been so long since he had seen them.

Mateo must be most a man by now, I wonder if he has married and moved away from Berks County. Mayhap he even has children.

He pictured a grown Mateo sitting somewhere in a cabin telling his children stories about their Uncle Jacob who had disappeared. The thought was very depressing, and he switched quickly to Hannah.

I wonder what she is doing this very night.

But thinking of her was even more depressing than thinking of Mateo, for he knew she was either a spinster waiting for a beau who would never return, or was already in the arms of another man.

Like he had done so many times before, he pushed the memories of them aside. Twas better to leave the past in the past.

He blew out the candle, and put himself to bed. But hardly had his head hit the pillow, than he heard, "Papa?"

"Shoshanna? Be yeh yet awake?"

He had not realized he had spoken in English until she also replied in English, "Yes, papa, I am." He heard her bed rustle, and saw in the dim light of the moon that she was sitting up, and staring at him. "Yeh need to take me home with yeh to yer brother and Hannah." She lay back, and curled up.

Jacob lay back also, but remembered his father once telling him, "A wise man should always listen to his wife and children, for it is through them that God often speaks."

Did God speak to me just now through her?

He had asked Him for direction, was this His reply? If it was, he must obey; he had promised he would.

He very much wanted to obey, to be able to obey. More than anything in the world he wanted to return to Mateo and Hannah. He wanted to go home.

And now, at last, he believed he could. If God had commanded him to return, He would provide a way.
Jacob fell asleep making plans.

19   New York

October 1774

"Look here, my liebkin," Jacob said, and lifted a weary Shoshanna into his arms. There spread out below them was at last the softly rolling hills of New York. It was a very pleasant sight after the weeks of forbidding mountains.

The first and major obstacle preventing his return to Berks County had been finally surmounted: circumventing the British army and its informants. As soon as they had passed east of Fort Pitt, he had been violating the boundaries they had ordained and faced the pursuit and execution the officer had threatened.

But, in his several years of exile, he had traveled the western territories extensively and had concluded the British traveled via, and controlled, almost exclusively the major rivers. They built their forts at natural bottlenecks through which most goods and travelers were forced to pass. Fort Pitt for instance controlled access to the Ohio River for the lands both north and south of it were mountainous and difficult to transit.

Difficult but not impossible.

Thus Jacob had simply chosen the most difficult terrain to traverse. He had gone as far south of Fort Pitt as he dared without encountering the hostile Indians of the south, and then went east over and through the mountains.

However, he had known the English had informants watching for settlers crossing the mountains; they had forbidden such crossings, so he could not simply continue over them. Instead, before he reached the spine of the mountains, he wended his way northeast until he was forced to again turn east by reaching Hodenosaunee lands. He had wished he could enter them, the traveling would have been far easier, but of course he could not.

Thus, the entire long weary trek made much longer by its circuitous route had consisted of conquering one massive mountain after another. More than once he had cursed himself for exposing Shoshanna to such an ordeal but she had proven herself to be far heartier than most four year old girls.

And now, that leg of their journey was behind them. Jacob was confident the hills below them belonged to New York Colony and the English would doubtless be reluctant to pursue him further even if they knew his whereabouts without informing the colonial authorities and this he did not believe they would do.

So he now faced only the warrant for his arrest for murder from Wynnewood and Miranda's reward if it was still offered.

Jacob considered, as he had often on their journey, remaining in New York and sending word to Hannah and Mateo in the hope they would come to him. The warrant of a town in Pennsylvania carried little legal weight in New York, although Jacob knew from his previous flight that did little to deter bounty hunters from pursuing him. Still, the law itself would not pursue him. He would be far safer.

But, as he had before, he discarded that plan; it simply did not feel right to him, although he could not say why. He felt compelled to return to Berks County.

He put Shoshanna down. "Another half hour," he promised her, "and we shall camp."

20   Can I Come Home

November, 1774

Jacob sat drumming his fingers on the table top listening to Shoshanna chatter with the inn's mistress, and tried to compose his thoughts. The paper he had requested from the mistress lay white and demanding before him. He had to write a letter to Hannah telling her he was coming; he could not simply show up after five years of absence; it would be unfair.

And he must do it now for at long last his return was imminent. He had not written before, because the challenges opposing his return had made it far from certain. There had been no reason to cause Hannah and Mateo to expect a return which might well not transpire.

He glanced at the wall where notices were posted. Among them was a post announcing the warrant for his arrest and a quite accurate drawing of his appearance five years prior. Miranda's reward was also very clearly posted. Jacob had seen them in many villages and at crossroads.

He feared staying in inns because of them, but they had reached lands where camping outside would draw unwanted attention; every bit of land seemed owned by someone and usually developed in some manner, so he had concluded an inn was the least dangerous option.

Still, his poster was but one of many, and thus far he had not attracted any unwanted attention. He was now so close to Berks County he could allow himself to feel confident he would return, and soon.

It would be unreasonable to expect things to have remained as he had left them, unjust to assume Hannah would welcome him back. Yes, she had promised to love him forever, but for long years she had not known if he lived or was dead. It would not have been unfaithful of her to give up hope of his return and learn to love someone else. And if she had, he did not wish to be an embarrassment to her.

But how could he learn the truth until he did return? He dared not risk giving her a return address and awaiting a reply; there was no certainty the letter would not fall into the wrong hands.

For that matter, how was he to explain his long silence in one short letter? He decided he could not; he would have to rely upon her to trust he had had no choice. He could only express his love and desire to now return.

He decided he should address the letter to her father instead of to her. If she was indeed involved with another, it would be best if she never knew he yet lived. An idea came to him; he could ask her father to leave him a signal somewhere which would indicate if he would be welcomed.

He dipped the quill into the ink, and poised it above the paper. Then he paused. How should he address him? Certainly not as 'father'. But they had previously shared a level of intimacy which required more than a usual salutation. He finally decided on, 'My dear Mr. O'Malley', re-dipped the quill, and wrote it.

Politeness and formality seemed to demand he ask after his health and that of his family, but Jacob decided he had not room upon the paper for such trivia.

Mr. O'Malley shall know I care for his health and welfare. But what should I write? What do you say to someone after five years of silence?

He decided to simply plunge in and state the facts; Mr. O'Malley had always valued directness.

'I am writing to inform you I hope to return within the fortnight. But I know not how things stand between us and between myself and Hannah. No more do I know Mateo's estate. I desire to avoid embarrassment to any of you. If my return would prove so, I shall forgo it, and I would ask you would never inform Hannah or Mateo of this letter. To that end, I request you give me a sign.

'There stands a great maple tree at the fork of the road some five miles north of your farm. I ask, if I would be welcomed, that you carve . . .'

What should I have him carve?

He thought quickly. It must be something unique, something which could not be there by random. He had it!

'A Star of David upon it.'

He knew Mr. O'Malley knew what a Star of David was, but suspected few others would. He believed himself to be the only Jew who had ever lived in Berks County.

'When I come, I shall inspect the tree. If the star is missing, I shall return to the wilderness without contacting you.'

He signed it simply 'Jacob Schram.' He did not think he should presume upon a familiarity which may no longer exist. He carefully blotted the paper, folded it, and, dripping a bit of wax upon it from the candle, scaled it. He wrote Mr. O'Malley's address, and handed it to the mistress.

It was not until she had borne it away that the fear struck him: what if the letter never reaches him? Letters often did go astray. But he shoved the fear away.

It is in God's hands; I shall trust him.

Then he wondered if he should have written that he was accompanied by a tiny girl. *No,* he decided, *that shall not matter. If they welcome me they shall welcome her.*

He looked down upon the girl. "Shall we go to our room?"

"Aw, Papa, do we have to?" She glanced at the mistress and her daughter as they waited upon the two other guests of the inn. Both the woman and the girl had doted upon Shoshanna.

Jacob hesitated. He hated to deprive her of their attention; he knew she not only desired it but needed it. It was good she was around women again. But he feared remaining for long in the public eye; someone might recognize him.

Marcella, the daughter, must have overheard their exchange, for she came to their table, and said, "Leave her with me. I'll tend to her, and bring her to yer room in an hour or so."

Jacob considered it. The girl was twelve or thirteen, easily old enough to be trusted. "Are yeh sure she would not interfere with yer duties?"

"Nah," she said with a smile. "T'would be a pleasure." She held out her hand to the child. "Do yeh want to come?"

Shoshanna glanced at Jacob who nodded, and Marcella led her dancing away.

Jacob watched them go with gratitude. As much as he adored Shoshanna, he realized he relished the thought of an hour of solitude.

He went to his room.

21   The Bounty Hunters

November, 1774

Jacob carefully squatted, his ears and eyes intensely probing the trees around him. He had left Shoshanna with Takawni hiding in a copse at the edge of the woodlot.

He knew the three men they had met that morning were tailing him. It could only be because they had recognized him, and were hoping to obtain Miranda's reward.

He sighed. It was frustrating to come so far only to be discovered almost at the end. But of course he had known the last leg of his journey would be the most dangerous.

Since beginning his trek, he had considered what his response should be if he were discovered. Should he kill to defend himself? He had concluded he should. Would not such killing be justified? And it was not as if he had not killed men before, for he had.

So why had he not killed these men pursuing him? Why did he not kill them now? He could do so with relative ease.

He did not know. He only knew he could not; not unless Shoshanna or he were actually attacked.

But if I do not kill them, how am I to rid myself of them?

He had decided to force their hand. *They surely must know I am in the wood lot. If they are intent upon capturing me, they shall have to come to me. Then what shall be, shall be. At least it shall then be a fair fight, not murder, and the confrontation shall occur out of the public purview and in such a manner that only I and my three combatants shall be endangered.*

But, instead of the subtle sounds of stalking, he heard suddenly a ferocious growl, a shot, a whine, and a scream. They had gone after Shoshanna instead. Jacob had not anticipated that;

only the most craven of cowards would abuse a child to obtain his end. He had given them credit for being more than that. Every fiber of Jacob's body strained to race to her defense, but he withstood the urge. Rash actions would get them both killed.

Instead he began a slow stalk toward her. He was again a Hodenosaunee warrior, silent, efficient, and passionately deadly. He would have no problem killing now, only in restraining his brutality.

"Jacob," one of them called. "Jacob Schram. We know who yeh be. We have yer wee gal. If yeh want her to live, yeh'll come to us peaceful like, with yer rifle held over yer head. If yeh don't . . . I swear we'll kill her. Yeh have one minute to show yerself."

Jacob had already discerned one of them, hiding behind a tree. *Fools, don't they realize they should be hiding on the far side of the copse? A second man is of course with Shoshanna, and the third . . .* Jacob probed for his location. *Ah, there he is, a mere five feet from the second man and Shoshanna. Cowards. The two fear being separated from one another?*

It was only too easy to slip around the first man and dispatch him with a knife to the throat. He died without a sound. Jacob slipped through the trees until the scene was open to him.

Takawni lay in a pool of blood. It was obvious from the torn sod surrounding him that he had died in agony. *Blasted incompetent oafs! They could not even dispatch a dog efficiently, without causing him undue suffering?* He had not thought his rage and bloodlust could be greater than it had been, but he now found he had been wrong.

One man stood with a knife at Shoshanna's neck while the other stood holding a rifle and scanning the trees fearfully.

Jacob knelt, and drew a careful aim upon the beast holding his daughter. He feared what the last man would do when his friend was killed; Shoshanna would be in considerable danger at that point, but Jacob expected he would attempt to attack him rather than her.

He fired; the man flung up his arms, unfortunately slicing the girl's neck and shoulder as he did so, and fell. The final opponent scanned the brush desperately, and fired his rifle wildly in Jacob's general direction.

Fool. He is now defenseless.

Jacob burst from the trees, and his tomahawk found its mark. It felt good to feel the skull crack, to see the blood spurt.

But then Jacob came to himself, and his bloodlust evaporated. He was not ashamed of what he had done; it had had to be done, but neither did he glory in it.

He went to his daughter, and examined her wound. Fortunately it was neither deep nor dangerous.

He froze. They were still not safe. He had sensed movement; someone was hiding behind a fallen tree some distance to their left. He grabbed his tomahawk, dashed to the tree, and leaped over it. But, in the midst of his leap, he saw who, or rather what, his quarry was, and withheld his blow.

It was but a child, a boy, perhaps eight or nine. *Who is he? He was certainly not with the three men; I would have seen him. He must be a local boy. But he poses a real dilemma. He has witnessed me kill those men. How much has he seen?*

If he saw enough, he must realize I had no choice. But has he? And will the authorities agree the killings were defensive and justified? Or were these men perhaps friends of theirs?

He groaned. *And, of course, the fact that I have a warrant on my head for murder already shall prejudice them. I cannot hope they shall fail to discover it. Then, even if they judge these deaths to have been justifiable, they shall return me to Wynnewood to face trial there.*

The boy was cowering beneath his dripping blade. Jacob knew he had to make a decision; it was his life or the boy's.

Every instinct within Jacob urged him to strike. One blow, and he and Shoshanna could escape. He was confident he could with ease cause any pursuers to lose their trail, but not if they could broadcast a description of them.

But he could not kill a boy.

So he turned the tomahawk, and offered it to the boy. "Take us to your father," he said, "and call your magistrate."

22   Behind Bars

November, 1774

Jacob sat behind the bars in the magistrate's house watching the boy, Benji, try to amuse Shoshanna. He had at least finally succeeded in getting her to stop sobbing. Although Jacob could not blame her for weeping. Every time he thought of Takawni lying dead, Jacob himself had to struggle not to cry. He had been a valiant and faithful dog.

It had turned out that Benji had not had to take him to his father and call the magistrate, for his father was the magistrate. And when the magistrate had heard that Jacob had spared his son's life, even at the risk of his own, he had been very thankful.

When he had asked his son to relate what he knew, Jacob had found the boy had witnessed far more than he had imagined. He had seen Jacob and Shoshanna slip into the wood lot, thought it suspicious, and, as a good magistrate's son, took it upon himself to investigate. He had seen Jacob conceal the girl with the dog in the copse, seen him go deeper into the woodlot, and seen the three men approaching. He had then hidden, witnessed the killing of the dog, and the abduction of Shoshanna. And he had related all of these facts and the subsequent actions to his father with surprisingly calm accuracy.

His father had gone to the woodlot to see the carnage for himself.

Jacob heard the door to the outside open and waited with trepidation. *Is this the magistrate returning? If so, what shall be his verdict?* He had to choke back a surge of panic. He did not like having his fate rest in the hands of a stranger.

It was indeed the magistrate. He could hear him speaking with his missus although he could not quite catch what they were saying. Shortly they entered bearing several plates of food, glasses, and a pitcher of water.

"Come, Sweet Pea," said the missus to Shoshanna, "yeh can eat wi' yer father." The magistrate unlocked the gate, and she swept in, and set the plates down on the small table of the cell.

The magistrate took a seat and considered Jacob. "I went and took a look at the scene," he said. "T'was just as yeh and Benji described it." He cocked his head. "Tis a wonder to me: yeh defendin' yerself agin the three o' em to once." He leaned back and again considered Jacob for a moment. "A right dangerous man, yeh be."

"Dern royalist brigands," the missus fumed. She lifted Shoshanna up to sit beside Jacob, checked the wound on the child's neck which she had earlier cleaned, and glared at him fiercely. "Yeh did us a good turn freein' us o' 'em."

"Wife!" the magistrate bellowed, "hold yer tongue. We don't know what his leanin's be."

"Ach," she responded mildly, laying out the pewterware. "Do yeh believe a man like 'im'd be a royalist? Look at 'im now."

The magistrate looked at Jacob and grinned. "Spect not." He grew serious. "Nonetheless, tis a dangerous time to be speakin' so freely."

Jacob had no idea of what they were talking but decided it was wise to remain silent.

Once more the magistrate silently considered Jacob. He finally seemed to reach a conclusion, and smiled. "But, as the missus said, few in these parts'll miss aught o' those three or fault yeh for defendin' yerself agin 'em. An' that's what I rule it— defendin' yerself. yeh'll face no charges from me."

Jacob nodded.

The magistrate sucked upon his mustache. "Still, I found this upon one o' the bodies." He reached into a pocket and produced a paper. Jacob recognized it as one of Miranda's posts. *Of course one of the men would have had a copy to justify arresting me had they succeeded in doing so.*

"It says here yeh're wanted for murder in Wynnewood." He looked up at Jacob. "Be that true?"

"I expect it is true that I am wanted."

There was a long silence and then the magistrate asked quietly, "Did yeh murder the man?" He referenced the paper. "Says here the crime was committed in '67. Yeh couldn't a been much more than a boy."

Jacob shook his head. "I didn't kill the man."

The magistrate pursed his lips, glanced at his son, and scratched his head. "Well now, this puts me in an awkward situation, that it does." He ran his fingers through his hair. "I'd like to believe yeh—I do believe yeh. Yeh spared my son when t'was not in yer interest; that aint the act o' a murderer. And Wynnewood—there aint a worse pit o' royalist vipers in the colony. T'would rankle me greatly to serve their interests. Still . . ." He sighed deeply. "I took an oath to uphold the laws o' the Commonwealth o' Pennsylvania, and those laws dictate I send yeh to 'em."

He looked at Jacob pleadingly. "Perhaps were yeh to tell me the particulars o' the matter, I could find cause to circumvent the warrant. Swear to me yeh'll tell me the truth, the entire truth, an' I'll believe yeh."

Jacob considered the idea. The magistrate seemed a fair and just man, and he was clearly kindly disposed toward him. But that was the problem; he was a just man, and Jacob could not tell him the entire truth without revealing Mateo's actions. And if the magistrate judged Mateo to be guilty of murder, he would consider himself obligated to bring him to justice.

But surely he shall not. Had Mateo not killed the master, the master would have killed me. Shall not the magistrate rule it a justifiable homicide?

But Jacob could not be certain he would, and it was a risk he refused to take. He would rather hang.

"That I cannot do," he told the magistrate frankly. "It would involve others who I shall not endanger."

The magistrate leaned his chair back upon two legs and considered him for several long moments. Jacob did his best to look back at him unflinchingly. Finally the magistrate dropped his chair back upon four legs and grunted, "As yeh wish." He rose and left the cell, locking it behind himself. Halfway across the room, he tousled his son's hair, glanced back at Jacob, and grinned. "Yeh've created a right dilemma for me, yeh know that don't yeh?" He turned away shaking his head. "Durned if'n I know what I ought best to do."

Jacob turned his attention to the meal set before him. It was still distressing to have his fate rest in the hands of another man, but he thanked God he had fallen into this magistrate's power. He was confident he could be trusted to deal justly with him and ensure he at least got a semblance of a fair trial.

Besides, he thought, *I returned at God's direction, He it is who delivered me into the magistrate's power. I must trust He had a reason.*

He took a healthy bite of the chicken leg he had been given. *And, the magistrate's missus is a durn good cook.*

23 Let's Make a Deal

November, 1774

The next morning, before the sun had fairly risen, the magistrate returned to sit outside Jacob's cell.

"I spent most o' the night wrestlin' with the dilemma yeh presented me with only to have my wife suggest the solution."

Taking care not to awaken Shoshanna who had shared his cot, Jacob rose and stood before him. "A solution?"

"If yeh'll have it." The magistrate sucked upon his mustache. "There's a provision in the law that a man who is serving in a militia is immune to a warrant until his service is expired." He considered Jacob out of the corner of his eye. "It so happens a force is being gathered to resist the advancement of a British army down the Mohawk River. They have a great need for men who are skilled in the forest to serve as scouts." He tipped his chair back against the wall, and grinned. "Based upon what I observed yesterday, tis a skill I'm confident yeh possess."

"But . . . why would we resist a British force? Would not resisting a British army be . . . treason?"

The chair thumped back to all fours, and the magistrate regarded him from under angry brows. "So yeh be a royalist after all. And yes, not resisting a British army would be treason."

"I do not even know what a royalist is," Jacob protested. When the magistrate looked at him skeptically, he added, "I have been in the west, across the mountains, for the past five years.

Since returning I have avoided any un-needed intercourse with people."

"Five years, eh?" The magistrate was again sucking upon his mustache. "Then yeh likely would not know what is goin' on, right enough." He looked up in surprise. "Across the mountains, yeh say?" When Jacob nodded, he said, "Aye, then yeh'd be just the man to be a scout for the general. T'would be a shame to waste such a man as yeh to a murder charge made by a pit o' loyalists like . . ."

He leaned forward. "See here, Jacob. The English have no right to send an army down the Mohawk River unless it has been requested by the colonial government. The river does not belong to the British; it is part and parcel of land granted by charter to us. The king himself has no right to violate the terms o' the charter granted us by a prior king."

"Pennsylvania?" Jacob asked surprised.

"No, New York, but those distinctions are meaning less and less these days, all o' the colonies are workin' together for the common welfare."

He eyed Jacob. "The question be: Will yeh serve the king, or the colonial authorities?"

Jacob laughed. "With the threat of death hanging over my head, the decision is clear."

The magistrate did not laugh. "Aye, tis clear and I'd not quickly take the word o' most men. But I rate myself as a good judge o' men and I make yeh to be an honest man. Yeh tell me yeh'll serve the colony in the militia, and I'll believe yeh. It so happens there is a man o' the militia in the village this very night. Agree to accompany him, and present yerself to General Benedict Arnold, and yeh'll be a free man."

"What about Shoshanna?"

"Is there no one to whom yeh could entrust her for a spell?"

Hannah, Mateo, or the Gerbers. But would it be just to simply drop in upon any of them and expect them to take her? No, he decided, *it would not be just.* Nonetheless any of the three would do so. He nodded his head.

"How long a journey would be required?"

"They are close. No more than a day, then we could turn north."

The magistrate nodded. "Yeh shall be allowed liberty to take her to them." He held out his hand. "Be yeh agreed?"

Jacob took the hand, and shook it. "Aye."

The magistrate grinned, and stood. "Glad I am to hear it."

But, when he tried to unlock the door, he found the lock was jammed, and would not budge. He looked at Jacob ruefully. "I guess yer stuck in there until I can fetch the smith."

"Did he build yeh these bars?"

"Aye."

Jacob grinned. "Yeh'd best tell him to temper his welds better. These hinge pin welds are so brittle; a boy could escape this cell." To prove his words, Jacob threw his shoulder against the edge of the door, both hinge pins snapped with a crack, and Jacob removed the door, and stepped out.

The magistrate had gone white. "How'd yeh know they'd snap like that?"

"I've done a bit of smithing in my day."

"Yeh knew it all along?"

"Aye."

"Yeh could'a escaped at any time. Yeh could'a killed us in our sleep.

Jacob nodded. "Could have, but didn't." He went to the cabinet where his weapons were stored, and armed himself. "Don't reckon Shoshanna and I could get a breakfast before we leave?"

24   Welcome Home, Son

December, 1774

They were very close to the tree where Jacob had asked Mr. O'Malley to carve a Star of David if he could expect a welcome at his farm. *What shall I do if it is not there?* He had not allowed himself to consider that possibility, but the time was fast approaching when he would have to.

God in heaven I beg it is there.

They approached the final bend and rounded it. Jacob sank to his knees and wept; he could not help it. There was not a star carved upon the tree. Instead dozens, perhaps hundreds, of stars, painted upon shingles, woven from vines, or fashioned from twigs, festooned every branch high into the tree.

"Lard o' mercy," exclaimed James, the private escorting him. "Would yeh look at that? I aint ever seen such a sight. What yeh reckon it be?"

Jacob could not answer, and only held Shoshanna and stared at the tree in delight. He finally stood with her in his arms, and grinned at the private. "Tis a wonder, aint it." He led the way south.

James stared at him quizzically, but followed without comment.

They were just approaching the O'Malley farm when there was a shriek, "Papa, he is here! Jacob is come," and a young woman came running from the shed.

Hannah? Oh how wonderful to see her again, but . . . this was not the reunion Jacob had imagined. But then he realized it was not Hannah; it was her little sister, Sarah. She had reached them, and Jacob swept her up, and kissed her cheek.

Then he held her at arm's length, and stared at her. She was blushing, he suspected because of the kiss, but she had not objected. "Sarah, yeh little imp, be this yeh?"

She nodded, and he realized she had indeed grown up. He felt cheated. He had always liked Sarah, and now he had missed some of the most interesting years of her life.

But Mr. O'Malley was come. Jacob stood for a moment unsure of himself, but the man drew him into an embrace, and slapped him hard upon the back.

"Welcome home, son."

"Thank yeh, sir. Tis wonderful beyond words to be home." He glanced at James. "If only I could remain. But I cannot. By God's grace, the day shall soon come when I may.

Mr. O'Malley stepped back. "Why may yeh not?"

"Tis the same problem, sir. The only way I could avoid being sent back to Wynnewood was to enlist myself to serve as a scout for an expedition to the Mohawk River. The private here," he indicated James, "is duty bound to deliver me to General Arnold without delay. I have no choice but to leave in the morn." He looked at the man and his daughter sadly. "I am truly sorry to do this to yeh."

Mr. O'Malley frowned. "Tis a disappointment that yeh shall not remain, but your return is a great joy. Why should yeh be sorry?"

Jacob drew Shoshanna to himself, and sighed. It would be best to get it over with. "Because I must beg yeh to do me an enormous service. This is Shoshanna. She cannot go with me to join the army, but I must . . ." *How do you ask a man to take your daughter for an indeterminate time?* He looked into Mr. O'Malley's face, and simply asked. "May I leave her with yeh?"

Mr. O'Malley gazed at the child for several moments, and she crowded back against Jacob fearfully. Finally the man soberly nodded. "Aye."

Jacob waited until he again looked at him, and then said, "She is not my blood, Mr. O'Malley. I have not been unfaithful to Hannah."

He stared into the wonderful and terrible grey eyes of the man until he nodded, and smiled. "I know that, Jacob. Have no fear."

Mr. O'Malley squatted before Shoshanna, and smiled at her. "She is very welcome." He winked up at Jacob. "Though t'would o' been better if yeh'd o' managed to bring me a boy instead." He smirked up at Sarah. "These durn females already outnumber me four to one."

Even James laughed at that, but Jacob could wait no longer.

"Where is Hannah?"

Mr. O'Malley stood and smiled ruefully. "Aye. Yeh would show up just now. Turns out she's not here, nor her mother or sister." He grinned. "They all be at the Williamson's"

"The Williamson's?" Jacob was disappointed. Hannah had known he was coming, he had thought she would have remained home.

"Yeh wouldn't know them; they moved into the area the summer after yeh left." He winked at Sarah. "Helped reconcile your brother to your absence."

"Helped . . . ?" Jacob felt lost.

Mr. O'Malley laughed, and put a hand upon his shoulder. "Come into the parlor, lad. Yeh too, private." He led them into the house. "Yeh've a great deal to catch up on, son, and little time to do so."

He indicated Jacob and James should sit. "Sarah, see what yeh can rustle up to eat, would yeh?"

The girl grinned, and offered her hand to Shoshanna. "Would yeh like to help me?"

Shoshanna looked up at Jacob, and he smiled encouragingly. "Go with her." She looked at Sarah, and then took the hand, and followed her out.

Mr. O'Malley went the cabinet in the wall, opened it, and poured them each a generous goblet of port. Handing them out, he sat, and considered Jacob with a satisfied grin.

Finally he said, "Yeh returned at a most auspicious time, my boy. Tis a sign o' God's hand. Yer brother is scheduled to marry Eliza Williamson in two days."

Jacob almost spilled his goblet of port. "Ma . . .Mateo? Married?" When Mr. O'Malley nodded, Jacob took a large gulp of the port. After a moment, he managed to ask, "What is she like?"

"Ach, yeh'll love her. Short, pert, and full o' energy. Hair as red as fire and a temper to match, but she loves yer brother heart an' soul. She is Hannah's best friend and Hannah is her Maid of Honor.

"When we received yer letter, yeh cannot imagine the joy it brought. We were worried we might have to delay the day, but it now appears we shall not have to. Yeh must know Mateo desires yeh to serve as his Best Man."

Jacob's heart sank, and he glanced at James. "But . . . I must leave in the morning. I shall still miss the wedding."

Mr. O'Malley was silent, and also looked at James. The poor lad squirmed uncomfortably and then said, "Yeh know, when I was with General Arnold at Quebec, we were captured by the English. I was imprisoned for some four months in a dank dirty cell. Caught myself the most awful fever. It still recurs from time to time." He grinned. "Less I miss my guess, I feel a spell comin' on now. I spec I'll not be fit to travel for a few days." He shrugged. "The general'll be pretty hot regarding the delay, but he'll know it couldn't be helped." He stood. "I think I'll step out. Give yeh a bit of privacy."

Jacob rose also, and shook his hand. "I do not know how to thank yeh, James."

"Think nothing of it. There are plenty of things more important than generals and war." He winked. " 'Sides, weddings generally mean a good feed." He glanced at Mr. O'Malley. "There shall be one shan't there?"

Mr. O'Malley laughed. "Yeh can bank on it."

"Then it'll be worth the wait." James again winked. "After my fever, I'll be hungry."

Sarah entered with a tray of bread, cheese, and sliced meat. Shoshanna had followed her in, and Jacob picked her up, and sat with her snuggled against his breast. James helped himself, making a bountiful sandwich, and stepped out.

Sarah set the tray between her father and Jacob. "Have yeh asked him? Is he gonna do it?"

"I'm thinking we should allow Hannah to ask him."

"Oh, aye," Sarah replied. She was regarding Jacob solemnly, but when he caught her eye, she grinned excitedly. "Then I best take yeh to her."

"Yeh had best think how to entertain Shoshanna whilst Jacob goes to Hannah on his own," declared her father. He laughed at her disappointment, and said to Jacob, "Tis not far. Follow the road west for perhaps a half mile, and yeh'll see a trail leading off to the north. That trail shall lead yeh directly to the Williamson's." He glanced at Shoshanna. "T'would be best to leave the child with us. Do yeh think she shall abide it?"

"Aye," Jacob said, and stood Shoshanna on the floor facing him. "Shoshanna, my liebkin, yeh remember me telling yeh of Hannah's sister, Sarah, and her father?"

The girl stared up at him soberly, and nodded.

"Then yeh'll know they be good people yeh can trust."

Shoshanna looked from him to Sarah and back. For a moment Jacob was a little worried; what if she was not willing to remain with them? But then Shoshanna's face broke into a smile, and she asked, "Be she the one who . . ."

"Aye," Jacob interrupted with a laugh. "That she be."

"Be I the one who what?" demanded Sarah indignantly. "What have yeh been telling her of me?"

Jacob winked at her roguishly. Despite the changes in her appearance, Sarah was still the little gal he had loved to tease.

"Only the truth, my dear." He looked back into Shoshanna's face, and grinned. Mr. O'Malley laughed.

Jacob took Shoshanna's shoulders in hand, and looked into her eyes. "Can yeh be a very brave gal and stay with Sarah whilst I go to see Hannah? I promise I shall return soon, and then yeh'll get to meet her too."

Shoshanna glanced at Sarah, and nodded, but then asked, "May I call her Aunt Sarah?"

"Why don't yeh ask her?"

Sarah beamed. "I've never been anyone's aunt before. I would like that." She held out her hand, and Shoshanna went to her.

Jacob glanced between the pair and Mr. O'Malley. "I . . . guess I shall go to find Hannah then." He started for the door, but Mr. O'Malley cleared his throat. Jacob stopped, and looked back.

"Perhaps t'would be best, Jacob, were yeh to leave yer weapons here. Yeh'll be meeting yer new sister-in-law and her family." He shrugged. "First impressions, yeh know."

"Oh, aye," Jacob agreed. He handed his rifle to Mr. O'Malley, and stripped himself of his other weapons. He felt naked and vulnerable, but knew the man was right; showing up armed as he had been would not have made a good impression. He looked at himself. He was rather dusty and very travel worn. "Mayhap I ought . . ."

"No," Mr. O'Malley said. "Hannah'll want to see yeh forthwith. None shall regard yer appearance." He grinned. "Go."

Jacob went.

25   Hannah

December, 1774

Jacob rounded a bend and the Williamson farm lay before him. He stopped and surveyed it. It was a pleasant and well planned farm, with the lane wending through a cow pasture and past a barn to a clapboard house beyond. He had not noticed a little lass collecting nuts in the tree line until she burst from it like a partridge, and ran with red pig-tails flying up the lane. He watched her go with amusement, and then followed her slowly.

As he came abreast the barn, he was suddenly accosted by a stout boy around twelve or so, also with bright red hair.

"I'll be asking yer business," the boy demanded.

This was not at all the reception Jacob had anticipated, and he stood for a moment taken aback, but then he saw himself through the boy's eyes. *I guess I do look rather intimidating. He is likely not used to wood runners. I cannot blame him for being on his guard.* In fact, Jacob found himself admiring the boy. *T'would take courage for a lad such as he to confront a man such as I.*

But there was the slam of the door of the house, and "Micah Ezra Williamson, just what do yeh think yeh're doing?" A young woman, clearly the sister of the former two, for she shared their red hair, was striding across the lawn. "Be this how yeh'd welcome a guest?" The words were flowing from her with a rapidity and volume Jacob could hardly believe. The very air seemed to crackle, and the boy slunk away.

The woman had reached Jacob, and stood appraising him. She was short, barely five feet, but she had a presence which belied it. *She must be Eliza*, Jacob thought, *Mateo's intended.*

She smiled, and literally took his breath away; she was almost shockingly beautiful. She held out her hand to him. "Yeh must be Jacob. Mateo and Hannah have both told me so much about yeh."

He took the hand, and nodded. "And yeh must be Eliza, my brother's intended."

She seemed pleased he had recognized her. She turned to the lass Jacob had seen run from him who was now peeping at them from behind a tree. "Luci, run and get Hannah."

But there was no need, for there Hannah was, running from the house. Before he realized it, Jacob was running also. And then she was in his arms; the arms which had ached so many weary days and nights for her embrace.

He was home, with the woman he loved.

He did not know how long they stood thusly, it may have been moments, it may have been hours, but when they parted, they were alone. She led him to a bench under a tree, and they sat.

"Jacob, you have finally returned!"

"I'm sorry it took so long, Hannah, I . . ."

But she had put her hand over his mouth. "I don't care why it took so long, Jacob. I only care that yeh are here, now." She smiled up at him. "We have a lifetime for me to hear yer reasons. Right now, I just want to enjoy yer company again and . . ." She smiled apologetically. "Reacquaint myself with yeh."

He cupped her chin in his hand. *God in Heaven, how I want to kiss her.* Instead he sighed, and said, "Alas, Hannah, we have but two short days." He looked away from her shocked face.

She reached up, and turned his face back to her own. "Then I shall go with yeh."

He stared into her grey eyes that he felt sure could see into his soul, and shook his head. "Yeh cannot. To be allowed liberty to come to yeh, I was forced to enlist myself into the militia. I must serve as a scout to General Arnold up the Mohawk River. But I swear as soon as I am free, I shall return for yeh; it'll be no more than a year."

She slowly nodded. "I'll be ready for yeh." Her eyes glistened, and she smiled. "Two days, yeh said?" When he nodded, she leaped up excitedly. "Then yeh'll be here for the wedding?" When he again nodded, she sat, and regarded him soberly. "Did my father speak to yeh of it?"

"He told me Mateo and Eliza are to be wed."

"Nothing more?"

He shook his head slowly. "He and Sarah hinted there was more, but yer father said it was for yeh to tell me."

She nodded, and swallowed before saying, "We, that is, Eliza, Mateo, and I . . ." She was staring at him almost pleadingly. "We're hoping we can make it a double wedding. That is . . ." She blushed, and stared hard at the ground. "If yeh desire to."

He sat shocked at the proposition. *Share a wedding with Mateo? Marry Hannah in two days? If I desire it?*

A slow smile spread over his face, and he gently lifted her face. "I do desire it." And then he did kiss her.

But then he pushed her away, and forced her to look him in the eye. "But there is something yeh must know first: I have returned with a wee lass. She is not my blood, but she calls me 'father' and I call her my daughter." He stared into her eyes for a moment. "I shall not—I cannot—abandon her. In fact . . ." He sighed, and added, "I must leave her with yeh when I go to join the general."

For the second time Hannah was shocked, but then she smiled. "I have always wanted a daughter." She laid her head against his shoulder. "I am so glad yeh have returned, Jacob."

26   The Weddings

December, 1774

Jacob sat, and watched his brother pace, and chuckled. Jacob's nature had always been to sit quietly when circumstances required it, but Mateo's nature had always required him to do something even when there was nothing to do.

Besides, the garments the two brides had compelled the brothers to wear made movement rather uncomfortable, especially in Jacob's case. He had been quite surprised when Hannah had presented him with a wedding suit, very nicely made, he had admitted, but somewhat tight for him. Like Hannah herself, he had filled out some since his departure.

But he had to admit Mateo looked very fine indeed in the suit Eliza had made for him. He still retained the silent grace he had always possessed, but he was no longer so scrawny, the hard cord like muscles had developed a bulk that was impressive. Watching them ripple beneath his dark brown skin was almost mesmerizing. His finely chiseled face had a Mediterranean cast about it which made it quite exotic, and he still had the mischievous eyes of an imp he had always had.

He realized Mateo had caught him staring, and was staring back.

"What?" his brother demanded.

"I was just thinking," Jacob said with a laugh, "yeh're nigh as beautiful as yer bride."

He received a quite painful punch on the arm for that, but Mateo also laughed, and said, "Yeh don't clean up so bad yerself."

Jacob wished they could just walk to the Williamson's on their own; they had had so little time together, and in the morning he would have to leave; the last thing Jacob desired was to be surrounded by people.

Yet they were alone for these few moments, and Jacob did not know what to say. There was so much he wanted to say, but how to choose which was the more important, and how to put it into words?

The rowdy sounds of their escorts approaching intruded upon them. Their time alone was almost over. Jacob put a hand on Mateo's shoulder, and said simply, "I'm glad yeh're my brother, Mateo. I'm proud to call yeh my brother. Even when there was a thousand miles betwixt us, knowing yeh were my brother gave me pleasure."

Without a word, Mateo enfolded him in a hug.

Durn fool, he always was one for hugs. What if the boys catch us like this?

But he returned the hug, and drank in every sensation, the feel, the sounds, the very smell of his brother. He did not know how long it would be before he would again be with him, and he intended to remember this hug.

And then the door was nearly beat off its hinges by Mateo's many friends demanding them to come.

In less time than it would take to tell, the brothers were being hurried down the trail in the midst of a rollicking band. Normally Jacob detested crowds, but he rather enjoyed this one. Everyone was jolly and spirited and they were all Mateo's friends. Being in their midst and watching them with him showed him aspects of his brother he had never before seen, aspects he liked.

Every man and boy except the brothers was armed with a musket, and they were fired without balls almost as fast as their bearers could reload them. And, although Jacob by nature preferred silence, he found himself being caught up with the revelry and exalting in the noise.

Very soon. they heard the sounds of shots and rowdy noise coming to meet them. That would be the male relatives and friends of the two brides. When they met, the two groups stopped, and Micah, Eliza's brother, shoved a lanky lad forth and said, "Here's our champion; where's yers?" Mateo clapped a hand on the back of one of his friends, and the lad stood forth.

It had been granted Jacob the honor of starting them. He took them to the edge of the crowd, and grasped each of them by the collar. "Ready?" he asked, and they each strained against his grip. He released them, and they sprinted down the road toward the Williamson farm to the salute of a dozen muskets and a multitude of encouraging or jeering shouts.

The two groups of boys and men mingled, and a lively speculation ensued regarding which of the two boys would win the race, and return with the jug of rum. Even though many of them did not know Jacob, they included him, and he was glad to allow himself to be drawn into the fun.

A great shout went up when the bride's champion was seen returning with the jug proudly held above his head. He was quickly received, and the jug made its rounds among the brides' friends until it was empty, which did not take long.

Then the brothers were surrounded by both groups, and marched to their respective fates, accompanied by a great many more discharges of muskets.

They were welcomed in the yard by Mr. Williamson, Mateo's soon to be father-in-law. Jacob liked the man. He was short, round, and jolly, with a very thick curly two inch fringe of black hair low on his scalp which had only a suggestion of white salting it. The remainder of his scalp was as shiny and smooth as if it had been polished.

Since it had been agreed that Mateo and Eliza were to be married first, Jacob, as his best man, stepped to Mr. Williamson, and demanded, "We have come for yer daughter, Eliza. Will yeh yield her to us?"

The man frowned, and answered, "I'll fetch the maid." He went to his house, and called for Hannah.

When she had come, the boys shoved Mateo to stand before her, and she inspected him with mock severity. "He'll do," she finally ruled, and led Jacob to Eliza's room. Hannah was so lovely Jacob found it difficult to play the part assigned to him as a best man; he wanted to simply sweep her from her feet, and carry her away.

But when he saw his brother's face as he escorted Eliza to him, he was glad he was the best man.

The wedding was not long, and soon Jacob found himself watching as his brother escorted Hannah to him. He was soon repeating the ancient vows, and listening as Hannah did the same. They were not Jewish vows, and this was not a Jewish wedding, but Jacob had reconciled himself to them: there was no congregation, there was no rabbi, there was no Torah, and Hannah was not a Jew.

But he had asked for, and had been granted, one concession. Just before the parson pronounced them man and wife, Jacob knelt before Hannah, placed her hands upon his head, and cried, "Ah-nee l'dodie." He stood, placed his hands upon Hannah's head, and cried, "V'dodie lee!" The Hebrew words, words Jacob had heard repeated in Jewish marriages of his childhood, seemed to hallow and bless their union, and he believed God approved of them.

The first words had meant, 'I am my beloved's,' and the second, 'And my beloved is mine.'
It was done. Hannah was finally, truly, his own and he was hers.

He had to struggle not to weep.

27 I am Iroquois

January, 1775

Jacob looked over the men gathered about the dozens of fires and struggled not to despise them. The militia was mostly composed of green farm boys and even greener city boys out for a lark. The first few days of their march, Jacob had laughed to hear them complain of blisters and sore muscles, but now he was tired of it. Were it up to him, he'd have sent most of 'em back to their mamas. He didn't envy the officer's task of trying to make men of them, much less warriors.

O' course most of the officers be pretty green and soft too. They've all of em lived life too easy.

There were however, a few dozen decent woodsmen among the militia, and Jacob found the fire around which they were congregated, and joined them. He had three rabbits and a 'possum and offered to share.

But one, a grizzled frenchie named Jean LaChapelle, asked, "Why'd yeh cut their ears off?"

Jacob cursed himself for the mistake. He had cut an ear from each animal, and left it where he had killed it purely from habit. It was an Iroquois custom to show respect for the animal and Teharonhiawagon who had made it. No animal was completely consumed, a part was allowed to return to dust as God had ordained. But doing so could identify him as an Iroquois, and Jacob had desired to keep that part of his history to himself. Iroquois were not well regarded in these parts.

"Yeh spend time with Iroquois?"

"Aye." Jacob knew the frenchies hated the Iroquois almost as much as the Iroquois hated them.

Jean spat a stream of tobacco juice in the dirt, and then stood with his hand on his tomahawk. "The damn Iroquois are filthy heathen fiends from hell!"

Jacob stood, and stared him in the eye. He knew Jean intended to fight him, and that the other men would despise him if he refused. Even the green boys watching from the other fires would. This was how many men and boys established themselves in a group. Cowards were universally scorned.

But the Iroquois did not brawl; they did not fight except to kill, and Jacob was afraid if he fought, his instincts would take over, and Jean would die.

So he instead lifted his chin, and said, "I did not only spend time among the Iroquois, I am Iroquois, a Seneca." It felt good proclaiming his identity, and he was filled with a fierce pride, and grinned at Jean coldly.

The effect of his announcement upon Jean was clear; the man was afraid. Jacob stepped toward the Frenchie, and Jean stepped back, and then fled.

The reactions of the other men were mixed; many showed open disdain, while some were regarding Jacob with respect. But it was clear that even those who respected him were uncomfortable with him.

Jacob went into the edge of the forest, and built himself a fire. As he skinned and began to roast the 'possum, he watched as Jean talked animatedly among the men, gesturing often in his direction. Clearly he was poisoning the other men's opinion of him. Jacob was confident he would no longer be welcomed by any in the camp.

He turned the 'possum over the fire, and told himself he didn't care. He was used to being alone; desired to be alone.

I only have to get this militia up the Mohawk River so they can turn back the British army ensconced in the fort, then I'll be free of my oath to the magistrate. I'll then return to Hannah and take her and Shoshanna into the virgin lands to the west.

He felt quite sure Mateo and Eliza would accompany them. Berks County was becoming too civilized and crowded for them too.

He decided to write a letter to them, and propose the idea.

28   Zachariah

March, 1775

"How's it go again, Jacob?"

Jacob looked at the little drummer boy, and laughed. "Aw, Zachariah, aint yeh got enough to keep in that head of yer's with all the orders yeh've been learning? I'd think with all of the drumming yeh're forced to do every day, yeh'd not want to touch the thing come evening."

For some reason—no one knew why—General Arnold had begun recruiting drummer boys. Every scout he had, including Jacob, were being sent out, sometimes to villages fifty miles or more off their path, to find, recruit, and return boys for his officers to train.

But Jacob welcomed the duty; he needed it to divert his mind from his estate. He almost wished he had never returned to Berks County. Seeing his friends, his brother, and Hannah again had been pure bliss, and his one night as a married man had been heaven upon earth, but it had made the weeks since then, especially the nights, hell.

Zachariah was one of Jacob's recruits; he had found him apprenticed to a wheelwright in a small village. When Jacob had announced he was looking for boys to volunteer as drummers, Zachariah had literally leaped at the chance, although Jacob had refused him at first. The boy was only ten, and Jacob had told him the general would not accept him, but he had pled so beseechingly,

Jacob had allowed him to return with him and take his chances. To his surprise, the boy had succeeded in convincing the general also. And he had become Jacob's shadow whenever Jacob was in camp.

Not that Jacob minded, few others in the camp would tolerate his presence because of his Iroquois past.

But the drummer boys were worked very hard; they had to learn the beats which would signal the various orders which might be issued in a battle, and the lieutenant assigned to teach them was exceedingly exacting. Which was why Jacob was always surprised that Zachariah wanted to learn Haudenosaunee drum beats at night.

But Zachariah just grinned up at him. "I like drummin'. Sides, Haudenosaune drummin' aint like military drummin'. I like usin' my hands instead o' the sticks."

Jacob dropped his pack and sat leaning against a tree. "Play me the victory dance for when the men return from battle, then." The boy began, and Jacob closed his eyes, and listened. The rhythms took him back; weary as Jacob was, he had to fight the urge to get up and dance. It felt good. The drum fell silent, and Jacob reluctantly opened his eyes and grinned at the lad. "That was well nigh perfect. Yeh need only to vary the pace and volume a bit more. Remember, I told yeh it builds to a crescendo and then fades back again?"

"Aye," said the boy, disappointed. "I tried to do so; was it not enough?"

Jacob was sorry he had disappointed him. "Yeh did it very well. I'm amazed yeh're able to get it so good having never heard it for yerself. But yes, the crescendo must be at least half again as pronounced."

"Teach me a new one Jacob, please. Teach me a war dance."

"Not tonight, Zachariah. I'm tired and I haven't et yet. Have yeh?"

The boy shook his head. "I've got the rabbits yeh asked me to guard though."

Jacob grinned and said, "Good. I'll teach yeh how to cook em like my sister, Silvathahae taught me." He winked at the boy. "You'll like em."

This was another reason he was glad Zachariah chose to hang around him The other men did not seem to understand that meat was far better after having been aged for a few days, and would either steal or throw away any meat Jacob tried to age. But now he had Zachariah to guard it.

He and the boy began to collect wood. Jacob was glad the boy had been distracted.

He had told Zachariah the Haudenosaunee had nearly a dozen different war dances, each of which were used before going into a different type of battle, but he had as yet refused to teach him any. Jacob did not wish to think of war and killing.

It bothered him a good deal that he was now a part of an army, and would doubtless be required to kill. He had promised the magistrate that he would serve in the militia; when he had made that promise he had known it would entail killing as well as scouting. He had agreed to it, and he would fulfill his promise, but his conscience did not rest easy with it.

He had no problem killing an enemy, he had done so in the past, but the English soldiers he would be killing were not his enemies; this was not his war. Indeed, despite the reasons the magistrate and others had given him justifying their actions, Jacob remained unconvinced.

Were not the English authorities the rightful rulers in the Colonies, and was not rebellion against them treason? Yes, he knew each colony had a charter which granted it rights which they felt the English were now violating, but did that justify war?

It did not help his conscience that the colonists themselves were divided on this same issue. The one truly distressing circumstance of his short return to Berks County had been the absence of his old master, Mr. Wallace. When he had inquired after him, he had been told sadly that Mr. Wallace had disappeared.

Jacob had always known Mr. Wallace was a proud Scot who was fervently loyal to the king. Hannah had told him Mr.

Wallace had very liberally expressed the opinion that the colonial congresses did not have the authority to oppose the king's will. Jacob had nodded when he had heard that, he could not have imagined his old master remaining silent. But Berks County was a Patriot stronghold, and there were many who had not taken the criticism lightly.

One night the smithy had erupted in flames. The fire had been extinguished, but Mr. Wallace had disappeared. Neither Hannah nor anyone else Jacob questioned knew if he was alive or dead.

Hannah and her family were Patriot, but Mr. Wallace had been their friend and they were as distressed as Jacob.

But now Jacob was a scout for a Patriot army. He looked over the men encamped about him; how did he know some of these very men were not responsible for the fire and his master's disappearance? For that matter, how did he know that when they engaged the enemy he would not find Mr. Wallace fighting among the English? What would he do if he did?

He shook his head. The odds of him facing his old master in a battle were very small, but the hard truth was that the men he would face would be men just like him; men loyal to the king. How could Jacob justify killing them? Only because he had promised the magistrate he would? He had made that promise only to save his own skin.

Some nights Jacob had trouble sleeping thinking about it.

Which was one more reason to be glad for the boy. Most nights Zachariah kept him telling stories of his life with the Haudenosaunee until they both were too tired to continue.

He put an arm around the boy's shoulders and gave him a half hug. "Tis glad I be to have yeh as my friend."

Zachariah just looked up at him with a grin and said not a word. He didn't need to; his eyes said a great deal. Jacob knew his apprenticeship had not been a pleasant one.

29   Free at last

April, 1775

Jacob stood, and waited for the orderly to announce his presence to the general within the tent. He wondered why he had been summoned. He had never before been ordered to appear before the general, always his orders had been given him by a subordinate. But the orderly soon reappeared, and told him to enter.

He found General Arnold sitting writing a report. He soon looked up, but then sat for a moment regarding him before speaking. "Jacob," he finally said, "I want to thank you for the service you've provided me these past months. I know you've done so out of duty only and that your heart is not with our cause."

Jacob was surprised, and a little alarmed; he had not spoken of his reservations to anyone, not even Zechariah. How did the general know of them?

But the general answered his unspoken question. "Private James McDonnel who delivered you to me had a letter from your father-in-law, Mr. O'Malley, in which he detailed your reasons for joining us." The general scowled. "I would normally not have accepted service from a man under such coercion; how could I be sure such a man would not betray us?" He grinned. "But your father-in-law was very convincing in his assurances regarding you, and I was in dire need of a man with your skill and knowledge of the north woods." He nodded. "I am pleased to say you have not disappointed me. For that I thank you."

He cleared his throat. "But we no longer are in need of your services. I am confident that our other scouts can lead us the remainder of the way, and I expect to find the fort deserted when we do arrive. Therefore I am discharging you."

Jacob was shocked. "That . . . is very gracious of you, sir. But . . ." He could not understand why the general would choose to release him before the task was completed. As much as he had longed to be free of his obligation, his sudden release was alarming. Miranda's warrant to return him to Wynnwood was still valid; when he was no longer in the militia, he would again be liable. Could it be the general was complicit in it?

No. He could not believe that.

But the general was again addressing him.

"Mr. O'Malley asked me if there wasn't something I could do concerning the warrant." He arched his eyebrows. "Turns out I have a friend who knows a friend who knows the mother of the current governor of Pennsylvania. Letters have been written on your behalf, and I am pleased to inform you this arrived among the other letters brought last night by the courier." He picked up a folded document, and handed it to Jacob. "It is the other reason I have chosen to release you now"

Jacob took and stared at the document, afraid to open it. He looked back at Arnold.

"Tis a full and complete pardon for anything you may have done in Wynnwood in '67, lad," the general said quietly. "You need never again fear their warrant."

Jacob was astonished. "Why would yeh do such a thing for me, sir?"

General Arnold stroked his chin, and smiled. "Your father-in-law has a great deal of confidence in you, lad, and he wrote a very passionate letter."

Jacob had to resist the urge to celebrate. Instead he saluted. "I thank yeh, sir. This means . . ." He had to swallow hard. "A great deal to me."

Were those tears he saw in the general's eyes? "You're welcome, lad. It gave me a good deal of pleasure to obtain it for you." The general picked up the report he had been working on. "The orderly outside shall have your discharge paper ready for you. You shall be free to go." He smiled. "Though if you should ever change your mind concerning our cause, I'd be pleased to have you again under my command."

Jacob did not know what to reply, and so merely again saluted, and then left. He was a free man, and could now finally look forward to beginning his life with Hannah. He could hardly wait to tell her.

30   Now It's My War

May, 1775

Jacob sat and contentedly watched his father-in-law teasing Zechariah as they roasted the plump turkey over the fire. General Arnold had released the boy from the militia with Jacob saying he had no further use for him and that the boy was too young to be left without supervision. Jacob had been happy to take him, and Mr. O'Malley had welcomed him.

"Yeh did as I asked," he had teasingly commended Jacob, "an' brought me a boy this time." Now they were getting acquainted, and it was clear that, despite his teasing, Mr. O'Malley was glad to finally have a boy in the family.

Behind Jacob in the house could be heard Hannah, her mother, and her sisters busily preparing a feast to accompany the turkey. Jacob felt rather guilty sitting idle while all around him labored, but it was all the O'Malleys would allow him to do.

He had shot the turkey early the morning he had arrived at his father-in-law's farm, and Mr. O'Malley had insisted that was to be his only contribution to the celebration. But Jacob could not long stand to simply sit idle, so he got up and told Mr. O'Malley he was going for a walk.

The walk did him good, although he felt odd and slightly vulnerable to be weaponless.   He was used to the weight and feel of his tomahawk at his belt and his rifle, shot bag, and powder horns about his shoulders. He grinned to himself. The last time he had been weaponless had been at his marriage. Except for that short lull, they had been his constant companions. But no more; he was done with weapons except for hunting.

He leaned against a tree, closed his eyes, and allowed himself to relive the afternoon before when he, Mateo, and their brides had discussed their futures.

Mateo had gotten his letter regarding the two families moving west and establishing themselves in the edge of the wilderness. Both he and Eliza had welcomed the proposal, and Hannah of course had also, although Jacob could tell she did not anticipate being separated from her parents. Jacob would miss them also, but there was no real future for either of them in Berks County, as even Mr. O'Malley had agreed. His father-in-law's one stipulation had been that he wanted to see his grandchildren at least once a year. Jacob had been very willing to agree.

Before Jacob had returned from the militia, Mateo had already taken a month, and scouted out several likely locations. He, Eliza, and Hannah had also begun to accumulate the necessary tools and goods they would require. Mr. O'Malley had acquired all of the smithing tools left by Mr. Wallace so Jacob would almost immediately be established in his trade.

Jacob's dreams were at last about to become true. By the next spring, the two families would be ready to make the move.

Three families, he reminded himself. Little Sarah, who was no longer so little, now had a beau, a fine young man named Michael. Jacob had met him on his former visit, and had liked him almost instantly. Then he had been introduced as merely a friend; Sarah had not intimated anything more, but almost the first thing Shoshanna had told Jacob when he had returned the day before was that the two were now engaged. By the next spring they would be man and wife, and Sarah had made it plain she and Michael intended to join the migration.

Jacob grinned; he had no objections certainly, he had always liked his sister-in-law, but he wondered what Eliza thought about it. When Jacob had first gone into exile, he had known

Mateo was rather fond of Sarah. He had encouraged the relationship, the idea of he and his brother marrying sisters had been a pleasant fantasy. It had been a bit of a disappointment to find him marrying another woman when he returned. Of course, once Jacob had gotten to know Eliza, he had welcomed her. Still, he wondered if Eliza knew of the feelings Mateo had once had for Sarah.

He wished Mateo were with him now, he would have enjoyed talking with him, but his brother had ridden to Wynnewood to invite the Sablonskis to the celebration the O'Malleys were arranging for the evening.

Just then he heard Zechariah calling his name. He answered him, and he soon appeared, gasping for breath, to tell him Mateo had returned, and wanted to see him. One glance at his face, and Jacob's heart was in his throat. Something was very wrong.

"What has happened?" he demanded, but Zechariah simply shook his head and whispered, "Hurry."

Jacob ran.

He was met in the yard by Mr. O'Malley who led him into the parlor where Mateo sat miserably waiting. The man left them alone, shutting the door behind himself.

Jacob dropped to his knees before his brother. "Tell me what has happened."

Mateo sat, and starred at him for several long moments, and then said simply, "Mr. Sablonski and Dick are both dead."

"Dead! How? Why?"

Mateo's face writhed, but he regained control of it, and said coldly, "Twas the English. They hung them for being spies for the Colonials."

Jacob felt cold. "Hung them?" Mr. Sablonski, the gentle and generous savior of his youth, was dead? And Dick, the only friend he had had during his awful servitude? And they had died in such a manner? He felt a wave of nausea sweep over him. "Were they spies?"

Mateo shrugged bleakly. "They may have been. They may not. I don't expect we shall ever know for sure." His eyes bored into Jacob's, and his face became livid. "The English themselves did not know for sure. The Sablonskis were not granted a trial; no evidence of their guilt or innocence was allowed to be presented." Mateo's face wavered, and he again struggled to regain control of himself. Then it grew hard. "The durn redcoats weren't concerned with discerning the truth, they needed to make an example of someone to put the fear of the king into the populace, and the Sablonskis were convenient."

Jacob stared back into Mateo's eyes, and he felt his own heart grow cold. The Haudenosaunee warrior within him rose, and Jacob welcomed it. *Now it is my war. Now I can kill.* He wished he had a redcoat upon whom he could vent his rage.

He buried his face into his hands. *But how am I to tell Hannah? She has already waited so long. How can I tell her she must wait longer?*

He felt a gentle nudge at his side. He looked up, and his wife enveloped him in her arms.

"Hannah, I . . ."

But she shushed him with a hand.

"I know," she said. "I shall wait for you." She smoothed his hair back, and smiled sadly. "For as long as it takes, I shall wait."

And then his tears came.

3 1   Ya Wanna Fight?

June, 1775

Jacob stood in the tavern with Levi Troyer and struggled to overcome his revulsion. He glanced at Levi and wondered how he knew of the place. Mateo had told him Levi was wild, but Jacob was dismayed to think any friend of his brother would frequent a pub such as this. The dirt floor was damp, the rum watery, the one window filthy, and the few candles smoky. Stench hung in the air and turned his stomach.

As his eyes adjusted to the gloom, he looked around at the men gathered within. He was sure he had never seen a rougher, less disciplined, or uglier group of men in his life. Most were drunk, few had all of their teeth, and all displayed scars testifying to violent encounters. He had little doubt anyone of them would be willing to kill for a trivial offense.

They were exactly the sort of men he was looking for.

As he stood and regarded them, he felt overwhelmed by the events of the past few days. Less than a week before, he had brought Zechariah proudly home to Hannah convinced he was done with war forever. Now he was seeking recruits.

The news of the ignoble deaths of the Sablonskis, the man and boy who had been Jacob's only friends during his long years of servitude and who had eventually saved him, had changed everything. Discovering that the British had hung them without a

137

trial simply because they were convenient victims to make an example of had made this Jacob's war.

The party which had been organized to celebrate his return had become instead a wake in the Sablonskis honor which had quickly somehow transformed itself into a militia organization meeting.

Jacob was still unsure just how it had happened. He had known Patriot ideals were strong in Berks County and that, although no one had been as close to Mr. Sablonski as he and Mateo had been, all of Berks County had known the man; he had been their tinker for twenty years and a frequent and welcome visitor. Still, the anger aroused by the news of his death had surprised Jacob and suddenly everyone had been talking of the need to organize a militia to avenge the murders, for such the Sablonki executions were considered.

In what seemed no time at all, Owen Knapp, the magistrate of the county, had written up a document and volunteers had been signing up. Soon it had had twenty names and Berks County had formed a militia.

But a militia needs a captain, and when the magistrate had asked who that captain should be, all eyes had turned to Jacob. He had been shocked and had tried to decline, but the men who had enlisted had refused to relent.

Finally Jacob had stood and addressed them.

"Before yeh men appoint me, yeh need to know what I'd be demandin' o' yeh, and where I'd be intendin' upon leadin' yeh." He had eyed each of them sternly.

He had been thinking on how the war ought to be conducted ever since he had decided to join it.

"Don't be expecting to get together once a week or so for a few hours to drill up and down the road and pretend to be an army. Nor even plan on taking a three or four month foray agin the English somewheres and then returning home a local hero."

He had paused and again looked each of them in the eye.

"I don't play at killin'. I know only one way to make war, and that's to go all out. Ifn, yeh make me yer captain, yeh'll be expected to do the same."

He had paused again to let that soak in.

"Now as to where I'd be leading yeh: yer fools ifn yeh think it'd be sufficient to drive the English from Pennsylvania Colony or even from all o' the colonies combined."

He had spat upon the ground.

"Yer fathers and grandfathers moved into this land and made a life for themselves. I doubt not most of yeh intend to do the same. But look around yerselves. How much land remains unclaimed? Enough for you perhaps, but what'll yer children and grandchildren do?"

He had let them think on that a moment, and then had pointed to the west.

"Across yonder mountains be a million acres o' prime land. Better land than this ever was. I've seen it. I've lived in it. There's the land yer grandchildren'll be settling."

He had again paused, and then said, "Ifn yeh don't want them to be subjects o' the King of England, yeh must take it from him, and the time to do so is now."

He had smiled at them grimly, and added quietly. "If yeh name me as the captain o' yer militia, I'll march yeh across the mountains. Yeh won't be returning for at least a year; mayhap longer. The only thing yeh'll have to live on will be what yeh can find, beg, steal, or kill. Yeh'll be hungry, thirsty, and in almost constant danger. And yeh best be prepared to fight, because I'll take yeh agin English and Injin forces twice, mebbe three times your size.

"But by Jamie, we'll take the west from the English and yeh'll have a thousand miles o' land to live free in; yeh and yer children, and their children after 'em."

He had indicated the paper laying on the table before the magistrate.

"Now that yeh know what it'll entail, yeh have this opportunity to either cross yer name offn the list or remove my name as the captain. I'll not think the less o' yeh either way. But ifn yer name is still there when the sun sets, an' my name is still at the top, I'll hold yeh to it."

He had turned, led Hannah away from the group, and they had taken a walk into the fields. When they had returned some twenty minutes later, he had found not one name had been scratched out, and ten more had been added.

Now, by Jamie, he had to make good his promise, and for that he needed men, a lot more men than thirty, and he needed men who were men. Thus his visit to the tavern. For a moment the idea of persuading these men to join his militia seemed preposterous; how was he to sell these hardened men on the vision of settlements in the west? What did they care for the future of children yet unborn?

But the longer he stared at them, the more his optimism revived. These were men who lusted for adventure, laughed at danger and hardship, and hated the English. And they loved freedom.

So he boldly stood upon a table, gained their attention, and made his appeal. He wasn't immediately thrown out which was encouraging, but neither did his speech seem to evoke much enthusiasm. He was about to step down from the table in defeat when a burly bear of a man pushed himself to the forefront.

Jacob was dismayed to find it was none other than his nemesis from Arnold's army, Jean LaChapelle. Jacob fell silent, and the Frenchie regarded him silently for several long moments. Then the man shifted the cud of tobacco in his mouth, and asked, "Who'd yeh have in mind to lead us?"

Jacob's heart sank. He knew Jean disdained him for being a Iroquois. And looking at the other men he could see Jean's opinion carried a lot of weight with them. He needed these men, and men they could lead him to, to have a chance of success in driving the English from the west. Was prejudice to doom the entire mission? He sighed, and admitted he, Jacob, was to be the captain.

Jean sent a stream of juice into the dirt, but then to Jacob's surprise, nodded at him, and said, "Then I'm in." Nearly every man assembled joined him.

32   Mr. O'Malley's advice

September, 1775

Jacob sat across from Mr. O'Malley, and admitted he was afraid. How he rued his hasty words. He still believed taking the west from the English was the right thing to do, and that it was viable. The English, he knew, only controlled a very few strategic crossroads; gain control of them, and he'd gain control of the entire territory. But how could he hope to be the man to do it?

He knew nothing of leading men, much less the innumerable details involved in providing for their needs. He would need logistical support, and a good deal of it. And once he succeeded in taking the forts of the west, they would have to be supplied and garrisoned; that would require official governmental support. Jamies breeches, he didn't even have official authorization for attacking the western forts, he only had the mandate of the Berks County magistrate.

Yet word of the expedition had spread though out the surrounding counties, especially among the less reputable class, and he had more than two hundred men awaiting his order to assemble and march.

He looked at his father-in-law, and weakly asked, "What am I to do with them?"

Mr. O'Malley said, "I think yeh underestimate yerself, lad. The men who've enlisted under yeh have more faith in yeh than yeh have. I dinna think yeh'd fare as bad as yeh presume." He smiled. "Nonetheless, tis true yeh've no experience provisioning for such an army, nor maintaining the discipline such an enterprise would require. Nor are there any among yer recruits who'd have the requisite skills or experience to compensate for yer lack.

"Fortunately I know of a man, the son of an old friend of mine, who has the opposite problem. He has the necessary skills and training, and moreover the required authorization from a Colonial government; the Congress of Virginia to be precise. But he lacks an army; my last letter from his father indicated he is struggling to raise one. I propose the two of yeh combine yer forces."

Jacob felt the weight of the world lift from his shoulders, and looked at his father-in-law with respect. *The man may laud me to the world,* Jacob thought, *but he is always two steps ahead of me, preparing my way.* Not for the first time Jacob thanked God for giving him such a man for a father-in-law.

"Who is this man?" he asked.

"George Rogers Clark," Mr. O'Malley replied. "He is a colonel in the Virginia forces and has seen a good deal of service. He is, by all accounts, a very able commander and, like you, believes the west is where this war shall be won or lost. I am confident yeh and he shall make a good team."

"But shall he be willing to share command? For that matter, can command of an army be shared? Would not one need to be preeminent?"

Mr. O'Malley nodded sagely. "Aye. And since he is the one with the experience and the authority, he shall command. Would that be a problem?"

"No." Jacob was more than willing to relinquish command. "I do not wish to command."

A frown escaped him. It was true, he did not wish to command, but . . . neither did he wish to be commanded. His old aversion to being bound reared its head.

But, as if reading his mind, his father-in-law put his hand on his arm, and said, "Like as not, bringing several hundred men to him will grant yeh a good deal of leverage though."

It is true, Jacob thought. He decided he would insist upon being allowed to enlist without binding himself to a term of service; he would be free to quit whenever he chose.

He looked up at Mr. O'Malley and grinned. "Where might I find this colonel?"

33   Kaskaskia

June, 1778

Jacob was called to confer with the colonel. He was glad; he needed something to distract him; he was missing his wife and daughter.

As Mr. O'Malley had intimated, the colonel had been exceedingly anxious to enlist him and the men he brought with him, and Jacob had succeeded in negotiating several concessions regarding his enlistment. Jacob would be free to terminate his enlistment at will; he would not be bound to any term. And he would retain the rank of captain and the men he had brought were to remain under his command. This last was at the will of his men, not at Jacob's will. He would have preferred to relinquish all command, but a number of his recruits refused to enlist if he did.

And, as Mr. O'Malley had predicted, the colonel and Jacob made a good team; Jacob was treated much more like an equal than a subordinate.

For some months being in the army had not been too trying. They had been spent scouting as the army marched across the mountains and through the forests of the west clear to the great river. Since such duties were very enjoyable to Jacob, especially as they moved into lands he had never seen before, although he had missed Hannah and Shoshanna, his days had been pleasant.

But since they had reached the great river and had been camping for nigh a fortnight he had had little to occupy his time. With nothing to distract him, the thought of his family being so very far away had become almost unendurable.

At least he had his brother and Zachariah with him, although he had done his best to convince the drummer boy to remain with his father-in-law. Mr. O'Malley had made it very clear that he was welcome, indeed that he was anxious for him to remain. But the boy would have none of it; he wanted to remain with Jacob.

And the separation was easier for Jacob than Mateo. Jacob had had only a few days with Hannah and so was used to being separated from her; Mateo had spent months with Eliza. And, just before they had left Virginia, they had received a letter which had informed them she was pregnant. Jacob often wondered if his brother regretted his decision to join.

When he reported to the colonel, he found him writing a report, but when the colonel saw Jacob, he lay it aside, and grinned. "The time has come for action. But I would run my plans before you and hear your council." He indicated Jacob should sit.

Jacob did so, and the colonel continued. "Most of the Indians in these parts are loyal to the English although they are not as yet hostile to our side. I believe they are loyal because the English supply them with manufactured goods and purchase their furs. Would you agree?"

Jacob nodded.

"And the primary trading post and the one which supplies all of the others in the district is Kaskaskia."

Again Jacob nodded.

"The English supply it by shipping goods down the rivers from Detroit." The colonel's eyes gleamed. "If we can but take the fort at Kaskaskia, we can supply it with goods shipped up the river from New Orleans."

"New Orleans? But is that not a French city?"

The colonel grinned. "The French have allied themselves with us. They have already agreed to supply us. If we control the supply of goods to the Indians will not their loyalty to the English be transferred to us? And if we control Kaskaskia, we shall sever the English from all of the territory south of her."

Jacob considered the plan and scowled. "I would be cautious trusting the French over much. It is not many years since this was French territory; how do yeh know they do not lust to regain it?"

Colonel Clark shrugged his shoulders. "I have been assured they do not. We have little choice but to trust them."

Jacob nodded. "As yeh will." He again considered the proposition. "Yeh shall certainly gain the loyalty of the Indian tribes if," and he emphasized his point by tapping his finger upon the colonel's desk, "yeh ensure they be treated fairly. Sell them quality goods at a fair price and give them a fair price for their goods." His eyes narrowed. "The Indians are not so ignorant as many whites assume them to be. Yeh sell them shoddy goods and yer entire scheme shall backfire upon yeh. Yeh'll earn their enmity instead o' their loyalty."

It was the colonel's turn to scowl. "What do you take me for? Do you really believe I would try to cheat the Indians?"

"No," Jacob answered. "Yeh would not, but yeh'll not be the man trading with them, shall yeh? No. It'll be someone yeh've appointed." He paused to let that sink in, and then added, "Take care whom yeh appoint and ensure he understands yer objective is not to turn a profit, it is to ensure the Indian's contentment."

The colonel nodded. "Your point is taken; I shall do so."

"And were I yeh," Jacob continued, "I'd ensure none but Patriots control the trading posts." He winked. "The French may be our allies and we may trust them, but let's ensure the Indian's loyalty is to us, not them."

The colonel considered him, and then grinned. "I think you mistrust them over much. But again, your point is taken. I shall ensure it is so." He leaned back. "But the key question is this: can we take the fort at Kaskaskia? What do you think?"

One of Jacob's duties had been to reconnoiter the fort at Kaskaskia, and he grinned. "The English garrison at Kaskaskia is not over large. Most of the population of Kaskaskia are Frenchies. I'd advise yeh to send Jean LaChapelle, and a few of our other frenchies to circulate among them. When they learn we're allied with France, and New Orleans shall be supplying us, I expect they'll welcome us and rally to our cause. My guess would be the English'll surrender without a shot fired."

* * * *

Jacob stood and scowled as the British Union Jack was lowered and replaced by Virginia's flag. Most of him was very glad his prediction of a bloodless victory had proven true, he hated needless killing, but a part of him was disappointed. A bloodless victory was not only boring, but unsatisfying, and it made him wonder if his exile from his family was truly needed.

Mateo especially could have used a good battle. He needed a fight.

34   Mateo's burden

December, 1778

Jacob glanced at his brother and sighed. The two were alone, returning from a hunting/recognizance trip and were each laden with meat.

Maybe he shall be willing to talk now.

Mateo had always seemed to revel in a good fight, and his quick temper was well known, but of late it had grown so volatile that even his friends, of which there were many, were avoiding him. Several had asked Jacob if he knew why.

Jacob had answered that yes, he did know, but that it was Matt's story to tell. Until he chose to share it, neither would Jacob.

It was December, and the last letter either brother had received from home had predicted Eliza would deliver in September.

Jacob looked at Mateo, and again sighed. *Why doesn't he just share what's going on inside?* But Mateo had not told anyone that he was even due to be a father, much less that the time was past.

Jacob made up his mind, and cleared his throat. "Do yeh wish to talk of it?"

His brother stared at the ground, but then muttered, "Aye." Yet he continued to walk silent for several long moments.

Jacob waited.

When Mateo did speak, it was not of Eliza but instead, "When yeh fled Berks County, Jacob, I was so miserable. So also was Hannah; I pitied her. But I never knew, never even imagined, what it was like for yeh."

He turned a haunted face to him. "How did yeh ever endure it, stayin' away when everything within yeh desired to return?"

He had taken Jacob by surprise, and he didn't know what to say. "I couldn't return, I told yeh that. I had been captured by the Iroquois."

"Yeh could o' returned," Mateo insisted, "before yeh were captured." He regarded Jacob shrewdly. "Yeh refused to do so, because o' the danger it would have meant to me." He stared again at the ground. "Just as I could easily return to Eliza, were I able to lay aside my duty." He grimaced. "I aint about to do that, but . . . 'tis a hard duty." He glanced again at Jacob. "How'd yeh abide it?"

Jacob again did not know what to say. He finally answered, "God gave me my Haudenosaunee family." He waited until Mateo again looked at him. "Just as He has given yeh me, and Zach, not to mention all of yer other friends. None o' us can take the place o' Eliza. But we can help yeh bear the separation, if yeh but allow us. Why don't yeh tell the others?"

Mateo just shook his head.

* * * *

But that afternoon, a large bundle of mail arrived, and was meted out. Mateo received a letter.

He took it to one side, and sat with his back to Jacob and Zach. After a moment, Jacob saw him hunch forward, and his shoulders begin to shake.

Is he weeping?

Jacob could not remember the last time he had seen his brother cry. He hurried over to him. Yes, Mateo was openly sobbing, but when Jacob touched his shoulder tentatively, the face which was lifted to him was beaming.

"Tis a gal," his brother whispered. Seeing Zach staring at them worriedly, he cried, "I'm a father! Me wife just had a wee gal."

The news took a moment to register, but the result was explosive and satisfying. Zach's loud 'hurrah' brought other men running, and the new father was soon in the midst of a crowd of celebrants. More than one bottle of whiskey was produced from a secret stash, and the party grew. Even the colonel showed up. Far from reprimanding the flow of alcohol, which was strictly forbidden in camp, he cheerfully accepted a bottle, and drank to the wee one's health.

"What's the babe's name?" he asked.

Mateo looked abashed, and replied, "I dinna know." He grinned his crooked smile, and shrugged his shoulders. "I dinna get that far in the letter."

"Well, finish the letter, lad," the colonel ordered. "We'll wait." He pointed his chin to a tree at the edge of the clearing. "Get on with yeh."

Mateo pulled the letter reverently from his pocket, glanced at Jacob, and went to sit behind the tree. Jacob understood the glance, and followed him. After a moment of reading, Mateo passed the letter to him, and said, "She doesn't have a name yet. Eliza wants me to name 'er. Any suggestions?"

Jacob shook his head. He would not have offered a name if he had had one. A child should be named by her parents. When he had renamed Shoshanna, it had been easy, the name had just come to him and seemed perfect for her. But how do you name a child you have never seen?

"I shall call her Sarah," Mateo declared. He grinned sheepishly. "I have always liked that name."

Jacob chuckled to himself. *He always liked the name because he always liked the gal.* But he resisted the urge to prod his brother regarding his suspicion, or express the worry Eliza might guess the reason and resent it, and only clapped his brother on the shoulder to acclaim, "Tis a fine name."

The brothers returned to the party and, for the first time in his life, Jacob allowed himself to become thoroughly and gloriously drunk. He was an uncle, and the desire to see the new child was enormous. Mateo's desire, he knew, was a thousand times greater. He wondered how his brother could bear it.

35　Injin War Dance

February, 1779

Jacob slogged on through the mud and rain with the 172 other men of the regiment. It had been a week since they'd left Kaskaskia and there had been a steady cold rain every day of that week, the ground was unfrozen, the mud was everywhere deep and miry, and every one of the men was miserable.

The colonel had done an excellent job of entrenching himself and establishing an efficient distribution of goods to and from the frontier trading posts and his expectation of the transfer of the Indian loyalty from the English to them had seemed to be confirmed. The supplies from New Orleans were arriving regularly and Jacob had to admit the French had proven courteous and loyal. Everything had been proceeding according to his plan.

But then the colonel had learned Henry Hamilton, the British commander in the West, had moved with a sizable force from Detroit down the Maumee and Wabash Rivers to the fort at Vincennes. In considering the motives Hamilton may have had for such a move, Clark had concluded he could not allow him to remain until spring. At that time the English would no doubt be resupplied and reinforced by Indians from the East with which forces the English commander could quite certainly quell the Western rebellion.

Colonel Clark had determined their only hope of survival, indeed victory, was to attack the fort at Vincennes before spring. Thus the miserable march through the rain.

Jacob wished the rain would turn to snow, and the ground would freeze. He did not believe it would be as miserable or as cold as this dreary frigid rain and mud. At least their packs would be dry. Each man bore a weeks worth of food as well as personal effects and weaponry; having it soaked doubled its weight. And the mud slowed their progress; already the men had been ordered to conserve their food. Short rations did not improve the men's moral.

Yet all understood the need to conserve. A boat had been loaded with ample supplies as well as six small cannon, sent down the Mississippi to the Ohio, thence it was planned to sail up the Ohio and then up the Wabash where it would meet the regiment. But until then, there would be no food but what could easily be shot as they traveled.

Quite suddenly the regiment drew up, stopped by a virtual sea of flooded plain before them. They had come to the Little Wabash which had overflowed its western bank by three miles. They knew it would have overflowed its opposite bank by at least another two miles. That meant at least five miles of frigid water varying from knee deep to hip deep with a swim across the river bed in the middle.

After a week of slogging through ankle deep mud and living and sleeping in constant cold rain, the flood seemed impassable. But Colonel Clark came to Jacob and said quietly, "We must cross. Have yeh any ideas?"

Jacob shook his head. "It shall take more than encouragement or threats to motivate the men to enter that water. A man would have to be crazy to do so." But he remembered that the war dances of the Iroquois had served that very purpose, to drive men slightly insane. He grinned at the colonel. "Get a good sized fire burning."

The colonel did not question his reasons, only ordered a fire to be built. It was not easy to build a fire in the wet, but the men were experienced in doing so, and it was not long before the regiment was gathered around it with steam rising from their clothing. Jacob called Zachariah to his side. "Yeh remember any of those Haudenosaune war dance beats I taught yeh?" The boy nodded.

"Follow my lead," Jacob told the colonel and Mateo. He stepped into the midst of the men and, fighting his self consciousness, stooped to dip his fingers into the clay and streaked it across his face. The colonel and his brother followed his example, and Jacob began the shuffling war dance of the Seneca. The war cry of the Iroquois rent the Illinois air.

None of the men had ever seen an Iroquois war dance, but many had seen or at least heard of other Indian dances, and Zachariah made his drum talk. At first slowly, but then increasingly quickly, men began to paint their own faces, and fall in behind them. Jacob began to chant one of the Iroquois war songs. No one but he understood the words, but all responded to their sounds. Soon the entire regiment was dancing; Jacob could see the rhythms and chants were having an effect. He increased the tempo and volume.

When he judged they had reached the appropriate frenzy, Jacob screamed his war cry, lifted Hannah over his head, and plunged into the flood of water. To his satisfaction, the regiment followed him as one man screaming their own defiance at the elements. The waters were exceedingly cold, but after a bit became bearable.

* * * *

Some hours later, the regiment struggled up a small hill to a wooded copse. Seven deer were found to have taken refuge upon the hill and were now trapped. The regiment made a cheerful camp, laughing over their dreadful ordeal, and teasing the young drummer boy for having used his drum to float over the actual river bed, instead of swimming. Zachariah, brave lad, made light of their jests; none but Jacob knew he could not swim.

Little time was wasted in slaughtering the seven deer, and placing them to broil over the dozen fires around which the men soon sat steaming.

Buoyed by having conquered the flood, with full stomachs, and warmed by cheerful fires, the men's spirits were high.

The difficulties still before them seemed trivial. Another few days and they would rendezvous with the supply boat, food would be plentiful, and they could use it to ferry themselves over the Wabash River even if it was also flooded. And when they reached Vincennes; well, they were confident they would catch them unaware and take the fort with ease. There was even talk of continuing their march to take Detroit itself.

36   Camp Hunger

February, 1779

Four days later the regiment reached the Embarrass River, nine miles from Vincennes. Wearily they marched along the river to its juncture with the Wabash.

But their supply boat, the *Willing,* was not there.

Even with careful rationing, the food was gone; less than a handful of parched corn per man remained.

Colonel Clark immediately had a log hollowed out and a crew of men appointed to search the river for the boat. A day was passed camped at 'Camp Hunger' as it was dubbed, but then the canoe returned with the news the boat was nowhere to be found. The colonel had to face the fact that they would have to cross the river and the nine miles of intervening flooded lowlands and then take on the fort without supplies or cannon. Added to that was the fact that he did not dare allow hunting parties to obtain meat, his planned assault could only succeed if he took the fort by surprise.

But these were hardened frontiersmen, they were used to privation. He ordered them to prepare to march upon the morrow and not one man objected.

Jacob was on sentry duty that evening when he spotted a boat come down the river. Moving quickly he took up a position along the bank where he had a clear shot at the men within and ordered them to land. When they did so, Jacob found he had captured five Frenchmen, and the Frenchies had a fresh killed deer. One deer for 170 men was not much, but it was meted out and the Frenchies were interrogated by the colonel. The colonel was happy to find the English had no suspicion of their presence. But they also told him Vincennes could not be reached without a boat; it would be impossible to ferry the entire regiment.

Jacob grinned at the colonel and said, "We crossed five miles o' flood in an afternoon, I expect nine miles in a day'll be doable." The Frenchies stared at him in disbelief, but the colonel nodded.

"We'll load our sick into the Frenchie boat and tow them along."

"But the boat shall founder if yeh load many more men into her," protested the leader of the Frenchies.

Colonel Clark grinned coldly. "You'll not be in her. You can walk like the rest o' us."

"Wade through that water? It'd be the death of us. It'll be the death of yeh."

The colonel regarded him with amusement. "You can either choose to wade along with us, or remain behind." He paused and then added, "But since I'll take no chance o' you betraying us to the English, you may be sure no one shall remain here alive." He turned to Jacob. "See they're well guarded until morning."

* * * *

Jacob stood behind a clump of brush on Warrior's Island and stared across the two miles separating them from Vincennes; the houses scattered up the hill, the timbered church and the long stockade of the fort with its five frowning blockhouses slowly rising into the setting sun. He turned and went to attend the meeting with the colonel to plan their assault. The men had eaten almost nothing for the past two days. He knew they would have to secure the fort very quickly so hunting parties could be sent out to obtain food. If they were fortunate, they would secure access to the village and obtain food there.

The colonel appraised him and the rest of the riflemen he had asked to assemble. "We have no cannon," he said. "The enemy do. But I believe you and your rifles can prevail.   In the morning I shall have you surround the stockade well beyond the reach of their muskets and wait in hiding. When the signal is given to begin the battle, I would have you shoot to kill any redcoat who shows his face over their ramparts. But you shall have to keep on the move. If they are able to locate you with their cannon, you'll face a round of grapeshot.

The remainder of our men I shall retain here and have them march in and out of the enemy's view to convince them we are a far greater force than we are. By God's grace we shall force Hamilton's surrender."

He paused to eye the riflemen. "But all shall depend upon your accuracy. Only by proving ourselves deadly shall we obtain their surrender." He turned to Jacob. "You, Jacob, I believe to be my most accurate shot and moreover the one who can get the closest to the enemy without detection. I shall have you commence the assault. The rest o' the men shall wait for your shot before firing." He regarded him piercingly. "And Jacob, make you first shot deadly."

Jacob did not like the idea of killing a man without a challenge, but nodded.

37 Attack on Vincennes

February, 1779

Jacob lay on his stomach in the mud where he had squirmed. *Thank God the rains have finally ceased, but lands-- this mud is cold.* He was much closer to the fort than he needed to be, but he knew the men with him were following his lead; they would get no closer than he, and he did not trust their aim to be as accurate as his own.

Why'd Clark have to name me as the one to commence the attack? How'm I to know the most opportune time? Besides which, despite all of his experience killing men, Jacob still found it difficult to shoot a man without a challenge. Once the first shot was fired, the challenge would have been issued, the enemy would be on their guard, t'would be a fair battle.

But not before.

However, an order was an order. There were several men who could be seen marching back and forth upon the wall of the fort, no doubt on sentry duty. Jacob wet his far sight, and settled it on one.

But at that moment a man came out of the gate of the fort leading a couple of goats, and carrying an ax. He led them to one side, and lined up the ax upon the neck of one of the goats. He raised it, and swept it down, but the goat was far too fast for him. Leaping aside, it wrenched the rope from the man's hand, and danced away.

Jacob watched in amusement as the poor man tried to catch the goat, dragging the second goat behind him. Of course he not only failed to catch the goat, but soon had lost the second. He called for aid, but instead men began to line the wall laughing down upon him.

Jacob had nineteen riflemen hiding somewhere beside him; he waited until twenty men were on the wall, then picked out one, and fired. Almost instantly the other rifles blazed. The butcher abandoned the goats, and ran for the gate, and Jacob counted seventeen bodies slumped over the wall.

Lands! How could three men have missed?

But there was little time for thought; the two goats were fleeing. One was coming his way. Leaping up, and ignoring the musket fire coming from the wall of the fort, he caught it, and tied it to a tree. At least Mateo, Zach, and he would eat well that night.

Dropping again to the ground, he slithered to a new position, reloaded Hannah, and searched the wall. The redcoats had not learned from their first lesson, there were a multitude of them standing quite brazenly, firing their muskets back at them. *Fools, don't they know they cannot reach us with those muskets even from the height of the fort?* He lowered his sight upon one, and killed him. There was a steady cracking of other rifles, and before Jacob could again reload, the walls were deserted.

After that, the battle, such as it was, became exceedingly boring. Only an occasional head would pop up, and then only for an instant. It took a quick hand and eye to hit one, but since each appearance was answered by a half dozen rifles, few escaped.

There was a dozen or so volleys of grapeshot from the cannon, but only two riflemen were wounded, and none killed.

In the mid afternoon, the gate suddenly swung open, and lines of redcoats ran forth, but several score of riflemen had been positioned for that very expediency, and the sallie very quickly failed, and was withdrawn.

Beyond that there was no excitement, and Jacob was very happy to relinquish his post to a replacement, take his goat, and return to camp to find his brother.

* * * *

The next day, Jacob was guarding the gate when it opened a crack to eject a solitary man bearing a white flag. The man was escorted to the colonel, and within an hour, Virginia's flag was being hoisted over the fort.

Jacob and Mateo stood together and watched the redcoats prepare to sail back to Detroit. Mateo did not think it was wise of the colonel to allow them leave to do so, but Jacob disagreed. "What would yeh have had him do? Line them up, and execute them? Take fifty men we cannot spare, and assign them to guard them day and night? Besides, twas the terms of the surrender. Had he not granted them safe and free passage, who's to say Hamilton would have surrendered?"

Mateo shook his head. "But allowing them all to return to Detroit . . . It'll make taking Detroit nigh impossible."

Jacob laughed. "Taking Detroit was impossible at any rate."

Mateo scowled. "We coulda taken it."

But Jacob shook his head. He had seen the fort at Detroit, Mateo had not.

* * * *

Jacob was summoned to the colonel's office. The month since their assault upon the fort had been grueling as Colonel Clark had acted swiftly to secure and reinforce their position. He had had no intention of allowing himself to be trapped within the fort as had the English.

"I am confident," said the colonel, "that we have broken the power of the English in the West irretrievably. While events may prove me wrong, I believe the West is secure. The same cannot be said of the east. Dan'l Morgan has been re-commissioned to command the 7th Virginia Regiment, but he needs good men behind him, needs em more than I. So, I'm sending you, Jacob, with your men to join up with him in the south of Virginia." He handed him a packet containing each of their enlistment papers, saluted, and dismissed him.

Jacob returned to his tent and asked Mateo to assemble the men of his regiment. While he awaited them, he looked through their papers to ensure all was in order.

All was not in order; one paper was missing.

Jacob ordered those men who had assembled to await his return and to ensure those yet not present to remain as well, and then he returned to the colonel's tent.

"What would you have, Jacob," the colonel asked.

Jacob cleared his throat. "I would remind yeh, sir, that Zechariah is one of my men."

The colonel looked at him for a moment. "The boy would be safer here," he said quietly. "You have my word I'll look after him."

"He would be even safer," Jacob said dryly, "had he remained at my father-in-law's farm in Pennsylvania. He refused to do so. No more shall he be content to remain with yeh."

A slow sad smile creased the colonel's face. "I expect you're right." He went to his pack, and found Zachariah's enlistment paper. Handing it to Jacob, he said, "I pray I do not live to regret this."

38   Dan'l Morgan

June, 1779

"'Hump it,' says he," Dave Elerson cried. "That's his middle name, Dan'l Hump-it Morgan. Why's he in such a gosh awful hurry?"

Jacob grinned and shrugged. He was too busy looking about himself. He had never been in this part of the country; he liked what he saw. It was far too settled for his taste, but he could see it had once been fine land.

Dave had been a pleasant surprise the day Jacob and his men had met and joined Morgan's Shirt Men as they were called. Nearly eight years had transpired since he had last seen the lanky Virginian whom he had beaten in the big rifle shoot, but the two had immediately recognized each other. Jacob was surprised for he knew he had changed a great deal while Dave had not seemed to have changed at all.

"I told yeh we'd meet again," Dave had greeted him.

Jacob was quite sure it had been he who had said that, but he had let it slide, and asked, "Do yeh remember me brother, Matt?"

Dave had glanced at Mateo, and grinned. "Be yeh the little scrapper who half killed the man who threw the rock?" When

Mateo had grinned, he had clapped him upon the back, and invited them both to share a bottle of rum he had in his pack.

When Jacob had indicated Zachariah, and told Dave he was also with him, the Virginian had nodded, and said, "Bring 'im along. Tis plenty for all." And Zachariah had shown a marked liking for rum.

Now, a month later, the three of them were swinging along through the North Carolina countryside following Morgan who was on his way to join General Howe to repulse the English armies ravaging the country. Jacob admitted he was setting a fast pace. He glanced to where Zachariah was trotting along with the rest of the drummer boys. At least it was easier for the men than for boys like them.

"Lookit him up there," Dave continued. "Yeh see how he glances back every ten or fifteen steps?" He grinned. "Yeh think he wants to see is he goin' too fast fer us? Not he! The ol' bastard's afraid he's going too slow. Someone's like to step upon his heels."

Jacob only grunted, and winked at Mateo. He liked Dave, but the man could talk the ear off a wooden Indian.

"Yeh reckon he thinks the battle'll be over afore we get there? Or perchance he never learned what a normal human pace be." The Virginian glanced back along the line of riflemen, and called out in imitation of the old man, "Hump it, boys."

The men howled in laughter, but up ahead Morgan glanced back, grinned, and noticeably increased his pace. The men howled for another reason.

John McBride, just behind the three, complained, "Goddam, Elerson, why'd yeh have to go and do that?"

Jacob glanced back, and grinned at him. "A brisk walk is good for yeh; gets yer blood flowin'"

"Easy for yeh to say."

"What do yeh mean by that?" demanded Mateo.

McBride apparently had not noticed the edge in Matt's voice for he replied, "I mean we aint all more Injin than white."

Mateo handed his rifle to Jacob, and slipped his pack from his shoulders. "Stop out."

"Goddam if I won't" the man cried, and in a moment the two were rolling in the ditch.

Dave grinned at Jacob, and the two stopped to watch. Jacob had grown used to Mateo's fights; he still did not like them, but no longer even tried to discourage them. He had used to rationalize that Mateo needed to fight to vent his emotions at being separated from his family; he now knew that his brother simply enjoyed a good fight.

He saw Morgan glance back, see the brawl, and call, "Fall out and watch the fun, boys." The men were happy to comply, and Morgan waited until the man Mateo was fighting was pretty much flagged before he broke it up.

"Who started it?" he demanded.

"I did sir," Mateo admitted.

"Yeh blasted critter! I'm gettin' real tired o' yeh trying to lick every man o' the corps."

"I started it," McBride said, but Morgan ignored him.

"I tell yeh, Matt, the next time yeh start a fight, I'll personally finish it. Yeh hear?"

Jacob watched his brother's eyes run up and down their commander's formidable body. Morgan had a reputation for his skill in a fight; a reputation no one had dared to challenge.

Morgan noticed it as well, and a grin appeared on his face. "Yeh think yeh can lick me?"

"No sir," Mateo said, but then his head cocked, and he grinned. "T'would sure give me pleasure to try though."

Morgan's weathered face flared in anger for a moment, but then he laughed. "By God, boy, I'll give yeh a chance one day. But right now we got us an appointment with the British." He turned on his heel and called, "Fall in men."

The line reformed, and the march resumed.

McBride reached up, and nudged Mateo. "I didn't mean to give yeh offense, Matt. Truth is, I meant it as a compliment."

"S'all right," Mateo said with a grin. "Twas a grand fight though, wasn't it?"

"Aye," McBride answered rubbing his sore chin. "That it was."

39   A bit o' Smithin'

June, 1779

That night a man came into camp asking if Morgan had a man who could do a bit of smithing. Jacob was called and asked if he wanted to take the job.

"What would yeh have me do?"

"We have captured a privateer ship which has been harassing and stealing from our merchant vessels. The crew is locked in the magistrate's basement, but they must be transported to Greenville for their trial and disposal."

"Disposal?"

The messenger drew his finger across his neck.

Jacob was a little shocked. "They shall be executed?"

"Aye, hung," came the cheerful reply. The messenger's grin faded as he noticed Jacob's revulsion. "These men deserve it. They've taken many an innocent life upon the seas and bankrupted more than a few honest merchants whose ships they plundered." The grin returned. "Besides, the greedy fools tempted their fate. Sailed their ship right up the Albemarle and Chowan after a juicy prize which had evaded them on the seas." He winked. "Got as far as Colerain and found a surprise awaitin' 'em."

"Aye," Jacob replied soberly. "But what would yeh have of me?"

"We've shackles enough for all o' 'em," said the messenger. "But the crew includes two who shall not fit the shackles; one is too large and the other too small. We need a smith who can cut one set o' shackles down and increase another. Can yeh do so?"

"Aye," said Jacob. "Yeh must know I've done no smithing for six years, but t'would be a simple matter o' cutting and welding. Is there no smith in yer burg who could do so?"

"We have a smith, but we don't trust him." The man looked around at them all. "The magistrate suspects he's a loyalist." He turned back to Jacob. "Will yeh come?"

"Aye. If the colonel releases me."

Morgan nodded. "We'll be heading north west on the morrow. Yeh can easily catch up with us." He grinned. "Yer brother has been boastin' about yer trackin' skills. I expect yeh'll find trackin' a regiment easy enough."

* * * *

Jacob waited for his eyes to adjust to the gloom within. Gradually the forms of the wretches became clear. The first to attract his notice was the captain of the privateers; he was unsure how he knew he was the captain; he simply did. Seated and standing, glaring at him, were the remainder of the crew. The longer Jacob looked at them, the more he felt many were familiar somehow, but it was not until he was brought to the two men he was to attend that he recognized them.

He saw before him the little demon, Arturo, who had given him so many undeserved bruises so many years ago, and the gentle giant, Isaac, who had tried to enable his escape. He was again among the very ship mates who had kidnapped and sold him into servitude!

He gazed again at the men surrounding him. There were many he did not recognize, but many he did; and the captain . . . he knew now why he had known instantly he was the captain. It was with difficulty he restrained his hand from his tomahawk. No longer did he pity the wretches; he almost considered asking permission to accompany them to Greenville.

When the captain stands on his gallows, shall he remember the day he sold a boy into twenty-one years of undeserved servitude in a similar square?
But he then looked into the sad eyes of the giant before him and sighed. *You great oaf, why did you not abandon this wretched captain and crew years ago?* He shook his head; there was nothing he could do; judgment had been passed. He sadly measured his old friend's wrists and those of Arturo's.

It was short easy work to cut a pair of shackles apart, shorten them, and weld them back together to fit the dwarf. It was nearly as easy to cut another pair apart and add metal to enlarge them to fit Isaac. It was when he began the process to weld them together the idea came.

He stopped and thought, but the decision was made in moments; he deliberately made a cold weld in each shackle. He was careful to beat the welds smooth and ensured there was no sign of a crack but he knew the center of the metal had not bonded. He then, instead of tempering the union properly, plunged the shackles into his pan of water.

He carefully inspected them. It was very plain to him the welds would never hold; it would be as plain to any other smith. *But if there was any smith nigh they trusted, they'd not have called upon me. And they'll be placed upon Isaac's wrists in the dark. Very likely they'll never be inspected closely.*

He grinned. *They'd better not be, and I'd best take care else they may break when I rivet them on him.*

He draped the two pairs of shackles over a shoulder, took up a hammer and an anvil, and returned to the prison.

He attached Arturo's shackles first. He took a sadistic joy in driving the rivets locking the shackles about his wrists firmly home; a joy of which he was both ashamed and satisfied. He sent the dwarf away and turned his attention to the giant.

He lay one shackle open upon the anvil and ordered Isaac to place his wrist upon it. The giant complied without a word. Jacob closed the shackle and shoved the rivet through the hole. He pretended to have trouble aligning it, leaned close to Isaac's head, and whispered in German, "Do you know how to swim, boy?"

"Eh?" asked Isaac.

"You asked me that nearly twenty years ago when you tried to save me from a life of servitude," Jacob said quietly, and glanced into his face.

Isaac stood blank faced and dumb for several long moments, and then understanding dawned.

"Jacob?" The man stared into Jacob's eyes. "Is that you?"

"Yes. I am Jacob, and I've not forgotten your kindness and mercy." He very carefully drove the rivet tight without jarring the welds. He turned the shackle so that the weld was uppermost, and traced his finger along it. "You see this discoloration?"

Isaac stared hard, but shook his head.

"You shall when they take you into the light." He lifted the man's arm down and placed the second shackle upon the anvil. "Take care with these shackles. Where the discoloration is the iron is as brittle as glass; one good blow and it'll shatter. You understand?"

Isaac placed his wrist on the shackle and nodded.

Jacob carefully placed the rivet and drove it tight.

The job was done. Isaac removed his shackled arm from the anvil, seemed to loose his balance, and fell against Jacob. "I'll never forget this, Jacob. God bless you." And he shuffled to his place upon the floor.

Without another glance, Jacob left. He hoped Isaac would make it to safety.

40   Jacob Quits

January, 1781

Jacob sat in a tree on a hill overlooking the marsh across which was an encampment of Redcoats. He often sat so; he was ordered to do so. Woe to any who ventured to sally forth; from such a vantage, Hannah could reach a great distance and, with constant practice, his aim was deadly accurate. He could not count the number of men, from countless encampments, who had met a sudden death by coming into his range.

He wished this campaign was like that with General Morgan when he had been in New York. Dave Elerson had been with him, and had told Jacob and Mateo of those days. Then they had fought battles. Now they skulked through the forests shadowing the English and harassing them but never confronting them. Jacob did not like these tactics; he would much prefer to face the enemy in an open fair conflict.

But he couldn't blame the general; he could tell he found the tactics as chaffing as did Jacob, but he had his orders just as Jacob did. Harass and cause attrition, but do not engage.

A rowboat slipped from the opposite shore and quietly made its way across. It had four men aboard; what were they doing? He watched until they were mid-marsh although Hannah could have reached them long before; he wanted to discover their intentions.

They stopped, and two raised eyepieces, and began to scan the shore while the others made notes; it was a recognizance team. A team which would never return.

Jacob wet the far sight and slid Hannah from the branches. He zeroed in upon the tallest of the men, Hannah barked, and the man fell flailing into the marsh. Two of the remaining three snatched up their weapons while the third searched the bank for Jacob.

He took his time reloading. He was not worried about their discovering him; they were armed with muskets, and he knew they could not reach him. Hannah slid forth again, and a second man went down.

The other two abandoned their search for him, and fell to plying the oars in an effort to escape. Jacob was not worried; they had a long way to go before they were out of his range. Another shot, and the third man lay in the bottom of the boat.

Hannah was almost too hot to handle, but Jacob reloaded her anyway. He had one more to finish the job.

But when he slid Hannah forth, he found the last man kneeling in the boat with his hands clasped in a mute plea for mercy.

The sight awakened him to the reality of what he was doing. He had just killed three men who could not defend themselves, and had done so calmly, almost nonchalantly. The realization sickened him. He eased Hannah's flint down carefully, and withdrew her.

He had no problem killing men in combat; men who needed to be killed. He had no problem with war; choosing a side and viewing those who chose differently as enemies. But this was not combat, and it was not war; this was killing; cold and calculating.

This is why I am parted from my beloved? Why I sleep cold and alone when I could be in her arms? Jacob grew angrier by the moment. *This is why I was not there to comfort Hannah when her father died?* The pain of the letter informing him of Mr. O'Malley's death was still fresh. *Why Mateo must fume in frustration because he has a daughter he has never met?*

This is why we suffer; to kill men in cold blood? Well no longer.

He slipped Hannah's strap over his shoulder, and climbed from the tree. He then walked straight to the camp, and into the tent of General Morgan; he knew it was a major infraction of discipline.

"Sir," he said, "I have come to tell yeh I have shot my last man in this war. I am going home."

The general regarded him calmly. "May I ask why?"

"I can no longer stomach killing men from ambush. Were yeh to fight, t'would be different. Yeh've riflemen aplenty to do what yeh're doing. Yeh have no need of me. But my wife does, and I have need of her. I am going home."

General Morgan steepled his fingers, and considered Jacob. "Yeh be right, o' course. I've no stomach for continuing as we are either." He paused for several long moments, and then asked, "If I promise yeh an engagement within a fortnight, will yeh remain?"

Jacob eyed him. "Yeh would disobey yer orders?"

The general grinned. "I would make a command decision to take advantage of auspicious conditions in the field which bode to our advantage."

Jacob grinned back. He liked General Morgan. "I shall await yer auspicious conditions."

41   Cat and Mouse

January 11, 1781

Several days later, Jacob and Mateo were called to the General's tent. They found him in a jovial mood.

"Jacob," said he, "I believe I have devised a way to accommodate yeh."

Jacob grinned. "An auspicious condition has presented itself?"

The general leaned back and said, "It may be more accurate to say I believe we can cause an auspicious condition to present itself. But I need a couple of volunteers for a sensitive and perhaps dangerous mission to set the scheme in motion."

"What would yeh have us do?"

"Are yeh in, Matt?" asked Morgan.

Mateo grinned. "Where me brother leads, I shall follow."

"Very good." The general leaned forward. "I intend to move the army to Grindal's Shoals on the Pacolet River today. Do yeh know where that is?"

Both men nodded.

"I want one of yeh two to find Benny's army, show yerself to one or two o' his scouts without letting them know yer doing so, and lead him to our camp along about nightfall. Do yeh think yeh could do that?"

"Aye," Jacob replied. He arched his eyebrows. "Yeh want the English army to know where we are encamped?"

General Morgan laughed at their faces. "Aye, that I do." He tapped his temple, and winked. "Trust me laddies, I've got it all planned out. Ol' Benny Tarleton is an able commander, and he's won his share o' battles, but he's predictable. I've got his number. I know what he's gonna do before he does."

He leaned back again, grinned, and pantomimed casting a fishing line. "Yeh boys set our hook, and we'll work him in to the side o' the boat, and before he knows it, he'll be in our frying pan."

Jacob didn't know how deliberately revealing their whereabouts to the enemy would result in their destruction, but he didn't need to, so he only nodded and said, "We'll set yer hook deep, sir."

But Mateo spoke up. "Yeh said what yeh'd have one o' us do. What shall the second do?"

"The second is to shadow the first and keep him alive just in case he runs into trouble." The general grinned. "I can't afford to lose yeh or yer brother."

* * * *

Jacob scowled at the man who was again standing and staring into the forests. Jamie's *breeches, is this the best the Redcoats have to offer? Tis no wonder we evade them with such ease.* He sighed, and once more screeched like an owl. That was the signal he and Mateo had agreed upon when Matt had lost his pursuer. Which he frequently did. Jacob was growing impatient.

Jacob saw Mateo show himself some distance away, but it took the scout nigh a minute to spot him. *Lands! It's gonna take us most of the night to lead him all the way to our camp.* Jacob was tempted to leave this one in the forest and return to the English camp to try to find a better tracker.

* * * *

Jacob was again before the General. As expected, as soon as the 'scout' had located their camp and returned to the English, Tarleton had mobilized his army and come after them. For the past four days, Morgan had kept his army on the move, and had kept a myriad of scouts busy making sure the English neither got too close nor lost their trail. Jacob had spent the night spying upon the English.

"And how is Benny and his army this morning?" was the general's greeting. "Be they still hot to catch us?"

"Colonel Tarleton is, sir. But I fear his army is flagging."

"Eh? And why is that?"

Jacob grinned. "I fear the English are not up to maintaining the pace yeh set, sir. They be marchin' most o' the day and into the night. They be unable to obtain food, and are running low. Their moral is low, and I doubt me Tarleton'll be able to drive them much longer."

"Ah, we cannot have that. Another day and I'll have them where I want them, but they must continue pursuing us. If anything, we want them hale and hearty. We want them to come at us full of confidence and enthusiasm. My plan depends upon it."

He thought for a moment. "We cannot slacken our pace; that is certain, else they'll catch us where we don't want to be." He grinned. "So I guess we'll have to supply 'em with some food."

"What?"

The general steepled his fingers, leaned his chin upon them, and considered Jacob. "Jacob, my lad, if yeh were an Englishman pursuing us, hungry, tired, and dis-spirited, and yeh came upon our camp in the morn which showed clear signs o' having been recently evacuated, with food still cooking upon a dozen or so fires, what would be yer reaction?"

Jacob thought for a moment. "I would be overjoyed at the bounty, want to eat it, but would be so excited that we had almost caught yeh unawares that I'd be loath to take the time to do so. I'd be eager to be on yer trail."

"Now put yerself in Benny's shoes. What would yeh do?"

Again Jacob thought for a moment. He knew the colonel was a disciplined officer who fought well organized battles. He would not want his men to rush into an engagement in a random place nor in a random order. "I would set up camp upon yer old camp, feed my men, and send out scouts to keep me aware of yer progress, but I would not pursue yeh. I would wait for yeh to roost somewheres, and then rouse my well rested and fed men in the midst o' the night, and march so as to engage yeh in the morrow."

Morgan slapped his thigh happily. "By Jamie, lad, I'll make a strategist o' yeh yet. That is exactly what he shall do, and exactly what I need for him to do." He waved him aside. "Go and get yerself some victuals and sleep. I've got some devising to do."

42 The Cowpen

January 16, 1781

The following night the riflemen, including Jacob, Mateo, and Dave, were called en mass before the general on a hill in the midst of the cowpen to which they had been marched the day before. The cowpen was not truly a pen; merely a wide parklike area where cows had been pastured

It was roughly 500 yards square, with a multitude of trees scattered through it but with no underbrush; the cattle had seen to that. There was the central hill upon which they were sitting at one end which fell away into a long dry swale which then rose at the end to face upon the Green River Road.

"This is it, boys," the general said expansively. "This cowpen yeh see before yeh is the objective we've been marching for this past week. This is the site where ol' Benny Tarleton shall meet his doom on the morrow or mayhap the next.

"The greatest part o' strategy is in choosing yer battleground, and this is exactly what we need for my plans. I've gathered yeh here to explain yer part in them. Unlike other units of the army, yeh'll not be under any commander until half way through the battle, I'll need yeh each to act independently as yeh see best, but yet in unison according to my plans.

"I expect on the morrow—early morrow, Benny'll have his army organized somewhere beyond the road yonder. When he is ready, he'll send an assault across the road and down upon us. He'll have two cannon in the center with a regiment of infantry upon each side and dragoons upon each flank. I want yeh boys to be in those trees awaiting him.

"When they come, I want yeh to ignore the cannon and the infantry, but take out as many o' the dragoons as yeh may. Concentrate upon their officers. One officer down is worth five or ten o' the regulars. Take out as many as yeh may but, and this is vital, I would have yeh fade away before the enemy reaches musket range. First, I don't wish to risk losing any o' yeh that early in the battle, but second, it is vital that they keep coming. I want yeh to decimate the dragoons and mayhap turn them back, but the cannon and infantry must be encouraged to continue. Yer seeming retreat shall do so.

"Behind yeh yeh'll find a line o' militia; mostly composed o' farmers and merchants. They are green and'll need yeh to buck em up. I'll have yeh scatter yerselves among them and continue to pick off the enemy. Again concentrate upon the dragoons; leave the infantry to the militia.

"But Jacob and Matt Shram, Dave Ellerson, Charlie Peterson, and Matt Ort, I'll have yeh in the center o' the line. Yer job it'll be at that time to take out the artillery men of the cannons. I'll not have yeh try to capture the cannons nor disable em. Take out the artillery men, and they'll be next to useless."

The general looked around at them all. "Yeh'll have to work fast for the militia shall have orders to wait until the infantry is within musket range, fire two volleys only, and then retreat. Yeh must retreat with them, and I want the retreat to appear to be a rout, not an organized retreat. Yeh understand?

"Until that point in the battle, yeh'll each follow my orders independently. But when yeh retreat the second time yeh'll find a second row of militia, this one composed of seasoned men. They shall be under the command of Lieutenant Colonel John Howard. Yeh'll fall in with them, and from that point forward be also at his command."

He paused, and looked them over. "Are there any questions?" There were none. "Very good, then. Scout out the terrain, and then get yerselves a good meal and sleep."

* * * *

Jacob was awakened the next morning by the general himself running through the camp shouting, "Rise up boys! Benny's coming."

He rolled from his blanket, grabbed Hannah and his ammunition, and stuffed a few biscuits from supper into his pouch; he might have time to eat them before the English arrived.

Some of the men displayed nervousness, but not Dave. "The Ol' Wagoner has never been beaten. He'll not be beaten now."

"Old Wagoner?" asked a man.

"Dan'l Morgan; the old man." Dave slapped the dust from his coon skin cap, and donned it. "Didn't yeh know he began as a wagoner in the French and Indian War? Worked his way up the ranks. An' he aint never been beaten. Yeh'll see. He's got the English just where he wants like he said. Now he's gonna whup 'em."

Jacob jogged between Dave and Mateo to take the positions they had each staked out hours before.

"Be it true the old man has never been beaten?"

Dave grinned at him. "He aint never been beaten since I joined him. Can't rightly say for before."

The tree Jacob had selected was on the edge of the road. Sure enough, although the enemy was not yet visible, there were clear signs of them roughly half a mile up the road. He grinned at his brother hiding behind a tree to his left.

This is it. I asked for a battle, and the Old Wagoner has delivered one.

He heard the militia taking their positions a hundred and fifty yards behind them. *Them farmboys don't know how to be quiet, do they?* But then he heard the English commence to march to beating drums and shrieking fifes. *So much for a surprise attack.*

And there they came arrayed exactly as the general had predicted.

If Tarleton had any sense he'd have waited another hour. The swale in which the militia waited was full of morning mists; even the trees where the riflemen waited was veiled, but the hill down which the English army marched was gloriously clear. *We hardly need the trees.*

The army was coming within Hannah's reach. *Focus upon the dragoon officers, Morgan said.* Jacob scanned the riders with their sabers brandished. *They sure are an awesome sight.* He picked out an officer, and Hannah barked. The man fell, but the line never wavered. *They are disciplined.* He reloaded as other rifles began to bark.

He shot again, and then retreated twenty yards to another tree. *The ol wagoner said to retreat when they reached musket range, but he never said how far.* He shot again. Still the English lines advanced. *This is nearly as bad as sniping from ambush.* But he knew he would soon reach the militia; then he would have to remain where the English could reach him with their musket fire. He did not anticipate being in such danger, but at least it would then be a fair fight.

He retreated once again, but this time hid in front of a tree instead of behind it. He wasn't worried about the English, he was beyond their range, but he was now within range of the muskets of the militia line. *It'd be just like one of those farmboys to get excited and fire in the direction of the English and plug me in the back.*

By the time he had retreated to the militia lines Hannah was so hot he was uncomfortable pouring powder down her muzzle, but he reloaded her anyway, and ran to the center to take on the artillery as he had been ordered. There were a good many gaps in the dragoon lines.

He had picked off two of the artillery men before the English infantry fired their first volley. He heard a ball whistle past his head. A militiaman two men away was lying groaning. Jacob understood why militia often broke and ran; being shot at was not fun. He had to respect the English who had continued to march forward in the face of their rifles which they could not reach.

They could reach them now.

The militiamen returned the volley. Scores of the infantry fell.

Jacob took out another artillery man. Indeed, he was not truly an artilleryman, only a common infantryman who had manned a cannon. There were no artillerymen left. *We're going to retreat after the next volley; I'll have to work fast.* But he could reload much faster than the farmboys and he shot twice more before they fired their volley and then he joined them in running to the rear.

He slid in beside a militiaman of the second line. Mateo slid in beside him.

"What's yer score?" his brother asked.

"Eight."

"Jamie's breaches! I only got five."

"There are plenty left."

Mateo did not answer, only slid his rifle up and shot. "Six"

The English were yet beyond musket fire; again Jacob was impressed that they kept coming with their beating drums, howling fifes, and shouts of 'halloo, halloo' against rifle fire they could not return.

Dan'l Morgan himself came riding down the line. "Form, form, my brave fellows. The battle is ours." To Jacob he called, "Give em an Injin 'halloo' back."

Jacob grinned, and the South Carolina air was rent with a Seneca war cry. It was answered by dozens of cries up and down the line from both riflemen and militia. The English had reached musket range, and the volleys resumed.

The difference between this militia line and the former was obvious. Not only could they load far faster, but while one group was loading, another would be firing so the English faced a nearly continuous fire. And, although the English were returning at least as good as they were receiving, the line did not falter. For the first time, the English advance was halted.

The two sides blazed away at each other for a few rounds, and then Jacob saw a regiment of Highlanders with bagpipes squalling sweeping down the hill. *Let em come.* They were nearly within Hannah's reach when he heard the drummer signal 'retreat.'

He could hardly believe his ears, and glanced to where Colonel Howard rode on his steed. *We could'a taken em.* But he was now under his command and so, with the rest of the militia and riflemen, he retreated up the hill.

But after only a few dozen steps the order 'about face' was sounded. When he turned, he saw the English had broken ranks, and were chasing them.

"Fire!"

He, along with the militia, fired point blank into the surging mass of men. He loosened his tomahawk expecting to hear the command to charge, but it never came. Instead he heard a volley from the left; off the English right flank. It was the Patriot cavalry who had swept from behind the hill to their position, dropped from their horses, and fired.

Almost immediately there was another volley from off the English left flank. It was the farmboy militia which had been regrouped and staged.

The English fell like a wheat field in a hail storm; not only dead and wounded, but surrendering men by the score who cast aside their weapons, and fell face down upon the sod.

In the rear Jacob spotted Colonel Tarleton himself riding to safety hotly pursued by Lieutenant Colonel William Washington, the commander of the Patriot cavalry. Washington overtook and unhorsed him. They were saber dueling hand to hand. But Tarleton was quickly joined by two of his officers.

Colonel Washington is a dead man.

But Washington's drummer, a black man named Hall, had ridden up; he leveled a pistol, and killed one of the officers.

Good lad. But he is now unarmed.

But Tarlton abandoned his surviving officer, and fled. Colonel Washington easily disarmed his foe, but not before Tarlton had reached the safety of his Legion Cavalry which he had held in reserve. Jacob watched as they executed a brisk retreat. The battle was over.

Jacob glanced at the sun. The entire battle had taken less than an hour. He still had his biscuits, uneaten. From his position half-way up the hill he could see the entire arena of the battle; it was littered with scores of British dead and wounded. Those who had surrendered were already being disarmed and lined up.

There were only a few fallen patriots. He had to hand it to the old man; it had been a superb plan and had been impeccably executed.

He quickly scanned the men surrounding him, and spotted his brother and then Dave Ellerson; they both appeared unscathed. He released a sigh of relief, but then heard an inarticulate cry from the far end of the field.

He saw the burly Frenchie, Jean LaChapelle, running toward a small figure sprawled on the ground where the first line of militia had taken their stand. A few feet away from it lay a drum.

Zechariah!

He was only five yards behind the Frenchie when Jean reached the boy, but Jacob stopped, and watched as the man knelt over him; he feared what he would see.

"How bad is he?"

Jean looked over his shoulder at him. "He's dead."

Jacob felt, more than saw, his brother and Dave arrive.

"Should we take him back to camp?" Mateo asked.

"No," Jean rasped. He indicated the pool of blood soaking the grass under the body. "This is his piece of God's earth; bought and paid for. Here he should stay."

Jacob agreed, and Dave said, "I'll fetch a pair of shovels; yeh fetch his things." Leaving Jean and Mateo to guard the body, the two jogged back to camp.

As Jacob gathered up Zechariah's small pack of belongings he felt sick. A worn wool blanket, a spare shirt, a ragged pair of breeches Jacob was sure were too small for the boy to yet wear, and a rabbit Seneca cape. Except for the cape, the lot was next to worthless. The cape the boy had made following Jacob's instructions during their long nights of idleness along the Illinois; it had been the boy's pride and joy.

Aint much to show for a life.

But then Zechariah had not had a long life; Jacob supposed he was no more than twelve. He thought back to when Mateo had saved his life when his old master had tried to kill him when he had just turned thirteen.

God in heaven, I hadn't even started to live.

He sadly picked his way back to where Dave was already waiting with the shovels beside Mateo and Jean.

They spread the boy's blanket out, gently carried the body to it, and wrapped it up. Then Jean and Dave each took a shovel, and began to move the bloody grass aside. Mateo and Jacob took their turns and, almost too soon, the grave was dug.

The brothers stood within it as Dave and Jean passed the blanket wrapped body to them. Jacob carefully folded the spare shirt and ragged breeches and laid them under his head. Then he and Mateo spread the Seneca cape over him, put his drum and sticks atop it, and climbed from the hole.

Jean took up a shovel, scooped it full of earth from the pile, and swung it over the grave. It hung suspended for a long moment, but then the great bear of a man flung it from himself, collapsed upon the dirt, and wailed like a baby.

Jacob had never respected the man more.

43   Base Villainy

January 17, 1781

As the sun began to slip below the horizon, Jacob was relieved from his duty guarding the English captives. There were over 500 of them. In the hospital ward were 200 more. In the dusk, scores of men were busy digging graves for the dead. The English had lost 110 men, the Patriots only 12 dead and 60 wounded.

He tried not to remember that one of the twelve had been the young drummer boy, Zechariah.

A list of those men whom the officers had recommended for commendation had been posted upon a tree. Jacob needed something to distract him from his thoughts and stopped to scan the list.

Hall's name is not on the list. It ought to be. His actions to save his colonel's life were as valorous as any of these listed. He understood the officers could not be expected to remember every action taken by every man in the army, yet it did seem odd Colonel Washington had not remembered. He resolved to bring it to the general's attention. The lad deserved his commendation.

When Jacob reached the general's tent, he heard voices from within but asked the orderly sitting outside it if the general could see him anyway.

"I'll check," the orderly said. He shrugged. "It's just a few of his junior officers, and they're only talking, not having a meeting." He disappeared within.

Jacob heard one of the junior officers say, "It gave me a quite a start to hear that Iroquois cry today. Now that those fiends are conquered, I had thought I'd never have to hear it again. Thank God it was one o' our own this time."

The Iroquois are conquered? All six nations? How can that be?

He heard the orderly ask if the general would see Jacob.

"Certainly, send him in," he heard the general say, and the next moment was ushered in.

"What's yer pleasure, Jacob?"

Jacob stared at him dumbly. *What?* "I'm sorry sir. Did I just hear the Iroquois confederation has been conquered?"

The general cleared his throat and looked away. "I'm sorry, Jacob. I know . . ."

The junior officer Jacob had heard talking interrupted. "Yeh heard right. We'll not have to worry about that menace; not for a long time, thanks to the generals John Sullivan and James Clinton."

"How," Jacob asked carefully, "did they conquer them? The Iroquois Confederation has withstood great forces; surely far greater than the Patriots could assemble whilst we are at war with England."

"Perhaps we should discuss this in private, Jacob," said Morgan.

Jacob looked from the general to the junior officer. "I'd hear it now if yeh please."

The general shrugged. "As yeh wish." He nodded to the officer.

"Why that was the ingenuity of the two generals," said the officer. He winked conspiratorially. "They did not engage the warriors. No, they waited until they were occupied elsewhere, and then slipped behind them to destroy their crops, burn their villages, and kill their women and children."

Jacob could not believe his ears, and stood thunderstruck.

The officer laughed. "When those fiends returned to find they had no food or shelter to return to, it broke em. Yeh can't fight if yeh're starving and cold." He nodded his head. "Right smart generals Sullivan and Clinton be. They did in seven months what the English and French both failed to do in two hundred years."

"Perhaps," Jacob said, "the English should imitate them." The officer kept grinning; he obviously had failed to recognize the malice in Jacob's voice, but Morgan had not. He was staring fixedly at Jacob, but Jacob continued, "I expect they'd bring us to our knees with little trouble were the militia to learn their farms, wives, and children were being destroyed in their absence."

The officer's face paled, but then he scowled, and said, "Taint the same thing. The Iroquois weren't but cold blooded savages."

Jacob's tomahawk was out and already descending when it was halted by Morgan's "Jacob!" Jacob slowly lowered it, and Morgan ordered, "Get out."

The junior officer rose from where he had fallen, and brushed himself off. "Yeh heard him, cur. Get out."

"I was speaking to yeh," said Morgan, and the officer appeared to note the malice in his voice, for he was not slow in obeying.

"The rest o' yeh, leave also."

They were left alone, and Morgan put his hand on Jacob's shoulder. "I'm sorry, Jacob. I wish yeh had not heard it like that."

"Be it true?"

"Aye, lad. I fear it is."

"Does the congress in Phily know of their actions?"

"Aye."

"What did they do to them?"

There was a long pause.

"T'would be best if yeh did not know, Jacob."

Jacob stared him in the eye. "Nothing was done to them?"

Morgan did not reply.

"They were commended?"

The general dropped his eyes. "Aye."

Jacob sank to a chair. After a moment he looked up. "This war is over for me. I'll be leaving to return to my beloved—this very night."

It was Morgan's turn to sink to a chair. "I don't understand. I expected yeh to be angry. I knew the Iroquois were yer people. But why . . ."

"I joined this war because two friends o' mine were hung for being spies. I could have tolerated them being hung if it had been proven they were spies; government agents have a duty to protect their government, but they did not receive a trial. I could not tolerate a government which could condone such an action, and I justified killing those in the English army because they were supporting it.

"But I have never known the English Parliament to condone, much less commend, a general who deliberately chose to avoid an enemy's combatants, and instead destroyed their crops, villages, and families, do yeh?"

Morgan refused to meet his eye, but answered, "No."

"Then how do I continue to kill Englishmen knowing their government is more noble than my own?"

There was a long pause. "I see yer point." Morgan eyed Jacob. "But yeh did not come here to resign yer post. May I ask why yeh did ask to speak with me?"

Why did I come? Ah, yes.

"I was reading the list of those who shall receive commendations. I did not see Hall's name. I believe it should be added."

The general frowned. "I fear I cannot do so."

"Do yeh not know what he did? Colonel Washington would be dead were it not for his actions; actions which endangered Hall's own life."

Morgan was again refusing to meet his gaze. "I know what he did."

"Then why . . ."

"Because it would not be the politic thing to do, Jacob," the general interrupted him harshly. He stopped, sighed deeply, and continued more quietly, "I must do what I must to keep this army together. Two thirds o' the militia out there would desert me were I to commend a black man."

For the second time that night Jacob had trouble believing his own ears. "But the declaration said, 'All men . . .'"

"I know what it says, Jacob."

"Then the words are not meant?"

"No government is perfect, Jacob. Governments are composed of men, and ideals often fail to be achieved."

"Aye, that they be." Jacob waited until the general looked at him. "But if a government is just and its rulers sage, they refuse to tolerate such failures."

The general nodded, but again said, "No government is perfect. There never was one, there never shall be. But this is the best we have. We must accept what is."

"Don't waste time fretting about what should be," Jacob again heard the Dutchman in his memory, *"the only thing that matters is what is."* But he rejected it.

That durn Dutchman was wrong. What is may not be what ought to be, but that only means we must strive to change what is. He could have and should have striven to change what was on my behalf, but he did not care enough to make the effort.

Mr. Sablonski cared, and he changed what was.

This government and every government shall be what it ought to be only if enough of its citizens strive to make it so, for there shall always be those who shall seek their own advantage by making it what it ought not be.

He held the general's gaze. "Be that as it may, this war is over for me. I'll be taking my leave this very night."

General Morgan considered him for a moment, and then smiled sadly. "Yeh cannot simply walk away from the army when yeh've a mind to. I cannot allow yeh to. Yeh signed an enlistment paper, and yeh must fulfill it. Yeh must remain for three months yet."

"If yeh check that paper," said Jacob, "yeh'll see it states I'd not be bound to any term. I may leave when I please."

Morgan shook his head, but called his orderly in and ordered him to find Jacob's enlistment paper. A few minutes later it was produced. He scanned it, and his face changed to surprise. "Colonel Clark agreed to this?"

"Yeh see his signature upon it."

"That I do." Morgan's face changed to a grin. "Well, then, it would seem I have no authority to detain yeh." He again called in his orderly. "Bring me a discharge form, if yeh please." The form was quickly procured, he filled it out, signed it, and handed it to Jacob. "Ye're a good man, Jacob. I'm sorry to lose yeh. God be with yeh in whatever yeh pursue."

"Thank yeh sir, twas a pleasure serving under yeh." Jacob saluted and turned to go, but at the tent flap glanced back and dared to ask, "How can yeh continue to serve, knowing what yeh do?"

The general looked weary. "A man does what he must, Jacob. Be gone if yeh would."

Jacob went to find his brother.

"Mateo," he said when he had found him, "I've come to say goodbye. I'm going home. This war is over for me."

Mateo nodded soberly. "I heard what happened; the fate o' the Iroquois, and how yeh overheard it. I'm sorry."

Jacob nodded. What was there to say? The Iroquois had chosen to side with the English against the Patriots.

He sighed sadly. "I wish we could return together."

He glanced across the dark field at the fresh grave he knew it held.

"Yeh and Zachariah both."

He eyed his brother ruefully. "The boy gave his all for the cause, and now I'm running off before the task is complete."

He shook his head sadly.

"But I cannot tolerate remaining in the service of a government which would commend such as was done to the Iroquois. I hope yeh can understand."

Mateo nodded, and put his hand on his shoulder. "Go Jacob." He grinned. "I'll be along in four months more or less; I'll trust yeh to have everything prepared. We'll move to the Ohio territory like we discussed, and leave all of this behind us."

Jacob grinned. *Leave it to Mateo*, he thought, *to find the one thing to say that could make me feel better.*

44   Jacob'r Children

February, 1781

Jacob had crossed into Pennsylvania when he heard the Seneca war chief, Cornplanter, was coming to meet with General Washington to negotiate terms of a lasting peace between the Patriots and the Seneca nation. It was the answer to his prayers.

Since hearing the fate of the Haudenosaunee, he had been desperate to hear news of his Haudenosaunee children, but he had not known how he could do so.   Surely this chief, of whom he had heard much, could tell him news of the fate of Dahayanduk, the village of his children. He had to intercept him.

He reached the trail he was sure the Seneca legation must traverse well before they were expected, and made a camp. Two days later the Senecas arrived, and Jacob was overjoyed to learn the chief known to the Americans as Cornplanter was none other than Gayentwahga, who had resided in a village not ten miles from Jacob's old home.

Oh! How wonderful it was to be in the midst of noble Haudenosaunee warriors again.

Gayentwahga recognized Jacob, stopped dead in his tracks, and then threw out his arms to welcome him.

"Techusin, is it really you?"

"Yes," Jacob said, going to him, and saluting him in the Haudenosaunee way. "What news can you tell me of Dahayanduk and . . . my family?" Now that Gayentwahga was here, he was afraid what he would hear.

The chief's face darkened. "You knew Dahayanduk was destroyed by the Patriots."

Jacob looked him in the eye. He hoped Gayentwahga did not blame him. "No. I did not know, although I feared it was one of those destroyed." He hesitated; he had to know, but he feared the answer. "My children?"

The old chief considered him sadly for a moment, and then said, "There were very few men in Dahayanduk when the Patriots came, but Atotarho led seventeen other young men and attacked the army as it approached the village; all were slain. But they held off the three hundred Patriots long enough for everyone in the village to escape into the forest. The village and all within it was lost, but not one child or woman was harmed." He put a hand on Jacob's shoulder. "Your son shall be long remembered."

Jacob did not trust his voice to reply. Memories of his son surged through him; the boy trotting before him in the forest, playing a violent game of lacrosse with reckless abandon, assisting his sisters with such surprising tenderness and compassion. But the memory which was most prominent was the memory of Atotarho turning back at the door for one last glimpse of Jacob; the pain and sorrow contained by his dignity. That was the trait Jacob most remembered of his son; his dignity.

The boy was barely sixteen when he lay his life down for those he loved.

"My daughters?"

Gayentwahga sighed deeply. "Ailantha succumbed to a fever the winter before the attacks. The Patriots had nothing to do with her."

Jacob felt as if the old chief were punching him repeatedly in the gut. *My baby gal is gone?* He knew she had no longer been a baby gal; she had been seven, perhaps eight, but in his memory she was still a tiny gal sucking on her hair as she played with his.

"Meilitha?"

He was relieved to see the old chief give him a bright grin.

"I am pleased to say she was healthy and happy when last I saw her." He clapped Jacob on the shoulder. "She has become a winsome and beautiful maiden. You would be proud of her."

Tears sprang to Jacob's eyes, and ran down his cheeks. He did not even try to hide them. "I always was proud of her." *Thank you, God; one of my children yet lives.* How he yearned to see her again.

But he knew it could never be. He had promised to never return to the Haudenosaunee lands, and the Seneca had promised to forever forbid him entry; the Haudenosaunee did not break their word. Unless, and until, the English released them from their promise, they would abide by it.

He wanted to give her something and, on an impulse, went to his pack, and withdrew the silver comb he had bought for Hannah. He had bought it from a silver smith in North Carolina when he and Mateo had first come to the East. Throughout their months in the South, he had relished imagining how lovely it would look in her hair; her delight when he gave it to her.

Hannah will understand. She will tell me I did the right thing; that it is what she would have wanted me to do.

He took the comb carefully to the old chief, and extended it to him. "Would you give this to Meilitha; tell her it is from me?"

The chief nodded soberly. "It shall bring her great joy to hear I have seen you, and that you are well." He considered Jacob. "You are well, are you not?"

"Yes." Jacob smiled. "You may tell her I am well. Tell her I have a wife and a child waiting for me, and am returning to them as soon as I leave you." The thought of returning at last to his beloved filled him with joy.

Gayentwahga smiled. "I am glad." He took both of Jacob's shoulders in hand. "May you live long and well, Techusin."

"Thank you," Jacob said, and then added, "May your negotiations with General Washington succeed in enabling the Seneca Nation to live long and well."

The old chief nodded. "We shall endeavor to make it so."

Jacob remembered that among a people renowned for their rhetorical and debating skills, Gayentwahga was acknowledged as exceptional. *That old general Washington and his advisors don't know what they shall be facing.* He almost felt sorry for them.

He wished he could prolong his time with the Seneca, but he knew they had many miles to cover, and he was anxious to conclude his trek to his beloved. So he was soon watching them make their way east while he rolled his pack, and resumed his walk north.

* * * *

In Philadelphia Jacob heard the news that General Morgan, a hero in all the Colonies due to his recent victory at Cowpens, had unexpectedly resigned his commission.

Good for him. I knew I had him pegged right. Perhaps his resignation shall prod some o' those in congress to do the right thing.

He shouldered his pack. He had intended to spend the night in an inn, but now found he could not abide the thought of spending the night in the city. Hannah and Shoshanna were awaiting him; if he pressed on, he would be in their arms by nightfall on the morrow.

End of book three: Jacob's Exile

End of Jacob's Struggle

The author very much hopes you have enjoyed reading Jacob's Struggle. He would be very grateful if you would be so generous as to post a review of this book on Amazon.com. Not only do such reviews enable others to decide if they would enjoy reading this book, but they provide valuable feedback to the author regarding his work.

If you would like to communicate with the author directly, you may do so at:

slabaugh.dj@gmail.com

or at:

Kinderi Publishing
2101 East M36
Pinckney, Michigan, 48169

He would love to hear from you, even if you have criticisms to offer of his work. (well intended criticisms are in fact valuable as they, more than any other mechanism, enable an author to improve his/her work)

The author will do his best to personally acknowledge and respond to each such communication. However he asks for patience as, at times, circumstances makes doing so difficult.

The first and last chapters of a considered fourth book:

***Jacob's Family*, has been included for your pleasure and (hopefully) anticipation.**

CHAPTER 1

Jacob ran his fingers through his hair, and struggled to remain seated. His sister-in-law, Eliza, had ordered him to stop pacing; they could hear it from within the cabin, and it worried Hannah.

"She has enough to worry about just now without yeh addin' to it."

God in Heaven what I would not give to take her place. But this was something God had ordained for women alone. He was so afraid.

The fear had taken root the moment Hannah had told him she was with child. But then it had been a tiny niggling worry, vastly overwhelmed by the joy the news had brought, and easily ignored. But, as the days had passed, and her belly had swelled, so too had the fear.

And now the day of reckoning had come.

He cursed himself for bringing her into this god forsaken wilderness.

It wasn't god forsaken at all, he knew. It was a very pleasant and bountiful land, a land both she and he loved, but it was deserted. Sarah, Hannah's sister, was expected in the spring along with her husband and two other families which were friends of theirs, but for now there were only the two brothers and their families for at least eighty miles.

And Eliza was not a true midwife.

Jacob wished Mateo was still with him, but someone had to milk their cow, feed their horses, and ensure Shoshanna was coping all right with Mateo's gals.

Hannah screamed. Jacob had never heard her scream except when she had been attacked by the bear; then she had been nearly killed. What must she be experiencing now to elicit such a shriek?

And he had to sit helpless.

He tried to remind himself that Eliza had had two children; she had survived them fine. And dozens of other women had also;

every human on Earth had had a mother who had endured this ordeal.

But some, like his Shoshanna, had mothers who had not survived.

With a start he realized he had not heard anything from the cabin lately. Was that good or bad? He stood, and stared at the door. *Why is it that fathers are always banished from the room when their wives give birth? It would be so much easier if I knew what was happening.*

The door opened to reveal a smiling Eliza.

"Yeh've a lovely baby boy, Jacob. Hannah is fine; the worst part is over." She frowned. "I tried to get her to wait until it was all over before calling yeh, but she would have none of it. She wants to show yeh yer son now."

"All over?" Jacob asked in a daze. "Yeh mean there's more yet to come?"

Eliza smiled. "Nothin' yeh need concern yerself about. She only needs to pass the placenta. T'will be a trivial task." She looked at him sternly. "Though I'll be askin' yeh to leave when that time comes."

He thought about asking her why he would have to leave, but thought better of it. His sister-in-law was normally a charming lass, but she was taking her duties as a midwife very seriously and, he suspected, would brook no opposition. So he just grinned meekly, and allowed her to lead him into the cabin.

His wife was beaming up at him proudly with a tiny naked child nestled in the crook of her arm. He glided over to them, and stared down in awe. He had a son.

"Isn't he lovely?" Hannah whispered.

Frankly no, he thought. But he remembered what Shoshanna's sister had looked like when she was born; she had been just as red, misshapen, and ugly. But Shoshanna herself was as lovely as a deer fawn. So he nodded his head. "That he is."

He looked into her eyes. "Be yeh all right?"

"Aye. Eliza said everything went perfectly."

"Yeh be not bleeding?"

She shook her head, and Eliza said soothingly, "She bled very little, Jacob. Yeh've naught to fear."

An intense look came into Hannah's face, and she strained.

"Ach, this is where yeh leave," Eliza demanded, pushing Jacob to the door. "The placenta is comin'."

She pushed the door almost closed, but hung her head out to say, "Don't yeh worry yerself. T'will be but a few minutes, and yeh'll be back with her. The hard part is past."

But then Hannah wailed, and Eliza slammed the door shut.

Jacob tried to be calm. *Eliza said there is nothing to worry about. Tis a trivial thing to pass a placenta.* But she had also said the hard part was over. *If so, why is Hannah again crying?* And before the door had slammed shut, he had caught a glimpse of Eliza's face. It had not looked like she thought everything was over.

Hannah wailed again.

He sank to the bench, buried his face in his hands, and prayed. *God of Heaven and Earth, I beg of You, do not take Hannah from me. Have mercy! Have I not lost enough?* He shuddered. He could not bear the thought.

He felt a nudge at his elbow. "Papa, why be yeh crying?" It was Shoshanna's voice. "I have never seen yeh cry before."

I am not crying, only praying.

But when he took his hands from his face, he found both they and his cheeks were very wet indeed.

He looked into his daughter's face, and saw she was terrified. He drew her into his lap, and enfolded her in his arms.

"It is all right," he whispered. "Everything shall be all right."

But she did not believe him, and began to sob into his shoulder.

He wanted to calm her fear, but did not know how.

How can I calm her fears when I am so afraid?

He settled for holding her tight, and rocking her.

He did not know how much time had passed when he finally heard the door open. He could not force himself to look up.

"It is all right," he heard Eliza say. "It is all over. Hannah is fine. She is asking for yeh."

He tried to get up, but Shoshanna clung to him. He sat back, hugged her to himself, and petted her hair, but said, "Yeh heard yer aunt, Shana. She said yer mother is fine. She wouldn't lie to yeh. Let me go."

His daughter looked at her aunt, and slowly released him.

Jacob looked at the open door. He was strangely reluctant to enter it. What would he find on the other side? Was Hannah truly all right?

Eliza laughed at him, and thrust him through it.

Hannah was laying in the bed with their infant still cradled in her arms smiling at him, but his attention was arrested by a mound of bloody sheets on the floor.

It was no wonder Yimsotha had bled to death; how could Hannah lose so much blood and live?

But Eliza shoved him hard toward the bed, and exclaimed, "Pay no mind to that, tis only the placenta, I should'a got rid o' it before I called yeh."

He turned to her weakly. "Yeh . . . yeh stopped the bleeding though?"

"Aye," his sister-in-law said gently. "Would I have told yeh she's all right if I hadn't? Go to her."

He turned to find his wife was laughing at him. He went, and sat beside her and stared into her eyes.

"Yeh truly are all right?"

"Aye," she whispered. "Very tired, but fine."

"Why . . . why did yeh have such trouble passin' the . . ." He glanced at the awful mound of bloody sheets.

He felt Hannah's hand gently turn his face back.

"Look at yer child," she commanded quietly.

He stared into her marvelous grey eyes. "I'd rather look at yeh."

"Look at yer child."

He tore his eyes away from hers, and looked at his son, but

. . .

How can that be?

He looked closer.

His son had turned into a girl.

He realized both the women were again laughing at him, and looked back into his wife's face.

"I don't . . . understand."

She laughed, and pointed with her chin at the crib in the corner. He followed her gaze, and saw a white mound with a tiny head at one end. He looked back at Hannah.

"Twins?" He grinned. "Yeh had twins?"

"We had twins," she corrected him.

Jacob turned back to gaze in wonder at his tiny new daughter. He felt a tremendous urge to hold her, and, without a word, Hannah lifted her up to him.

He stared into the babe's eyes, and her face contorted, and then resolved itself into a smile. Jacob's knees almost collapsed, and he turned and sank down to sit beside his wife.

His daughter had his mother's smile. It had been oh, so very many years since he had seen his mother's smile. He bowed his head over his daughter, and wept.

"I hate to interrupt," Eliza said gently, "but it is not good to leave her naked for too long. I think it would best if I were to wrap her up, and put her with her brother."

Jacob reluctantly relinquished the child, and Hannah said, "I'd see my other daughter if yeh please."

Eliza paused. "Be yeh sure? Yeh need to rest."

"I wish to see her."

"I'll fetch her," Jacob said, and went to the door.

When he opened it, Shoshanna jumped up, and stood staring at him fearfully.

"Be she all right?"

"She is," he answered, and held out his arms.

She leaped into them, and asked, "Do I have a brother or a sister?"

He stared into her beautiful eyes, and smiled. "Come and see."

He carried her into the cabin, and together they leaned over the crib.

She stared into it a moment, and then looked at him with shining eyes. "Twins?"

"Aye," he said proudly, "a brother and a sister both."

She squirmed from his arms, and reached to touch them; her new brother grabbed her finger, and held on. "A brother and sister both," she whispered in wonder.

"Aye," Jacob laughed. He was growing used to the fact. "Yer mother is too efficient to waste her time producing only one."

"Ha," Eliza retorted, "Yeh aint foolin' me, Jacob Schram!" She knelt beside Shoshanna, and put her arm around her. "I expect this was yer father's doin'." She smirked up at Jacob. "I expect he just couldn't stand the thought o' yer uncle Matt and me havin' more'n he. He had to find a way to bypass us."

Shoshanna ignored her aunt's teasing, and looked up at Jacob. "What are their names?"

Jacob could only stare back at her in confusion.

He heard Eliza laugh, and ask, "Yeh mean yeh haven't picked out names yet?"

Jacob grinned at his sister-in-law, and shrugged. It was embarrassing, but . . . he had been so worried about Hannah's welfare that such a mundane task had never occurred to him.

"Their names are Atotarho and Ailantha," Hannah declared.

Jacob went, sat beside her, and took her hand.

What a woman she is. She knows what it means to an Indian to honor their dead in this way.

He did not trust himself to speak.

Still, I cannot allow her to name them that. They shall spend their lives among whites; they need white names. And they shall be surrounded by Indians who despise Iroquois; they would recognize the names as Iroquois names. I would not have them burdened by that prejudice.

And there was another reason even more important: he suspected it had cost his wife a good deal to suggest naming them that. Hannah missed her father very much and, though she had never said so, he believed she desired to honor him by naming her first born after him.

He leaned over and kissed her.

"Atotarho and Ailantha shall be their middle names. Their first names shall be Robert and Luella."

He watched as several emotions fought for possession of her features, but they finally resolved themselves into the most beatific smile he had ever seen.

"Do yeh know how much I love yeh, Jacob Schram?"

"Almost as much as I love yeh, Hannah O'Malley Schram."

Hannah giggled like a young girl, and then turned to Shoshanna.

"Shana, my love, can I have a hug? Tis the first time I've seen yeh all day. I've missed yeh."

Their daughter ran to the bed, and threw her arms around her. Jacob grinned to see the worried look on Eliza's face, but the woman said nothing.

"I'm so glad yeh be all right," Shoshanna whispered.

Hannah caressed her back, and frowned up at Jacob. "Were yeh worried?"

The girl nodded, and Hannah gently pushed her away until she was looking her in the eye. "Well yeh can worry no longer. Yeh can see I am fine."

Shoshanna nodded soberly, and then smiled. But she then turned to Jacob, and demanded, "Why don't I have a middle name, Papa?"

He shrugged. "I don't know. I never considered it." He sensed it was important to his daughter, and took her shoulders in his hands so he could look her in the face. "What would you like as your middle name?"

Shoshanna glanced at Hannah fearfully, but then asked timidly, "Yimsotha?"

Jacob nodded, and smiled. "I am sure your mother would be very pleased."

Hannah reached up, ran her fingers through Shoshanna's long raven hair, and agreed. "Both of yer mothers would be pleased."

CHAPTER ??

July 4, 1817

The speech droned on.

Why am I here? I hate this.

Jacob glanced up the hill to where Hannah sat. She had chosen to remain in their cabin and watch from afar. She shared his aversion to crowds; especially festive crowds. He wished he had been able to remain with her. *She's likely laughing at me. How*, he wondered, *did Luella convince me to be a part of this fiasco?*

But a glance at his grandson's face reminded him why he was there; Lil Jake's face fairly shone with pride for his pappy. His pappy and great uncle Matt were to receive medallions from the great Senator McKinley himself. The boy did not understand how little either his pappy or his uncle Matt enjoyed this charade; this was a big day for him. Jacob determined he would not ruin it for the boy. He forced himself to sit quietly, and pretend to listen.

The pompous fool of a senator was prattling on about Matt and Jacob's daring exploits and the many British and Loyalist men who had been felled by their rifles. Jacob did not care to be reminded of the men he had killed. He was, however, amused to hear some of the exploits attributed to him. He leaned over to whisper in Matt's ear, "These sure be excitin' stories. 'Most makes me wish I'd'a been there."

Matt snorted, but covered it with a cough.

Jacob sat prim, and stared soberly ahead as the senator laid out another whopper and Matt struggled to maintain his dignity.

The senator finally concluded his introduction, and Matt and Jacob stood to receive their medallions. Jacob glanced at the sun. *Only an hour and a half to introduce us, not bad for a politician.*

The senator reached up, and hung a silver medallion on a string about his neck saying, "For your valiant service, please accept this medallion from a grateful nation."

A grateful nation. What does that mean anyway? How can a nation be grateful?

He glanced at James, the senator's black slave. *Is James grateful? Aint he a part of the nation? But for what does he have to be grateful? For that matter, are the widows of the men I killed grateful?* He reckoned not.

How many were there; a hundred? Two hundred? He didn't know.

What has their deaths wrought? He stared at the senator. *The ability of pompous fools like this to believe they're more important than they are?*

He felt like ripping the medallion from his neck, but instead turned, and sat. He just wanted to get this ceremony over with.

But the senator was not finished. "After the war," he intoned, "Jacob continued to serve. Savages far and near learned to fear his Hannah's roar."

Jacob felt Matt's hand on his knee urging him to restraint, but he shoved it aside.

"The name of Jacob Schram shall go down in history as the greatest Injun kill . . ." The speech was cut short by Jacob's hand on the senator's shoulder which spun him around to face him.

"Some of the finest men I ever knew was Injuns," Jacob hissed. "Some of my best friends too." He glared; inches from the man's eyes. "I never killed a Injun I didn't have ta; and aint no man ever accused me of bein' a Injun killer." He paused to let his words soak in. "Ifen yeh all want ta stay on my good side, yeh won't start now." He released the senator, and sat.

The senator brushed his coat nervously, and turned back to the crowd. "As I was saying," he said, "Jacob Schram shall go down in the history of Ohio as its greatest . . . er . . . defender of innocents." The crowd roared its approval. The man swelled like a cock, and strutted about the platform.

"And now," he said, "Mr. Schram has graciously agreed to demonstrate his fabled marksmanship for us." He indicated a fence some twenty yards to his right. "Mr. Schram shall stand behind yon fence and shoot into the square upon this post." And he pointed at a six inch square slab nailed to a post on the left front side of the stage.

"I thought yeh wanted an exhibition of marksmanship," Matt burst out. "Jamie's breeches, a child could do that!"

The senator turned waving his arms. He came over to them, and whispered, "We didn't want to risk a miss." He glanced at Jacob. "He is not as young as he once was; his eye . . . er . . . his hand . . . that is . . ."

Matt's fists clenched, and his face was red, but Jacob reached over, and squeezed his leg. "Be at peace, brother." He glanced at the senator. "Be yeh ready for the demonstration?" When the senator nodded, he lifted his rifle, and strode calmly to the fence.

The senator said a few more words, and then moved to the back of the crowd.

"What'ch doin' back thar?" Matt mocked, "Yeh could see a sight better here." But, despite the laughter of many in the crowd, the senator declined to return.

Jacob considered the slab of wood for a moment, and then called Lil Jake to him. He gave his medallion to him, and told him to prop it atop the slab. The boy ran to do so. It shone in the sun, and made a fine target. He licked his finger, wet his far sight, and slowly brought Hannah to bear. He paused to relish the moment, then slowly exhaled, held his breath, and gently squeezed. Hannah barked, and the medallion fell.

Lil Jake ran to retrieve it. He held it up gleefully, and cried, "Dead through the center." He ran with it to the crowd, and showed it proudly. "Dead center," he said again.

"Le'me see that," his uncle Matt called. The lad leaped upon the stage, and showed him. Matt examined it, and turned with a grin to Jacob. "The boy's right," he called. "Yeh couldn't'a drilled it better if'n yeh'd used an auger."

The crowd was impressed, but apparently Lil Jake heard some muttering regarding it having been a lucky shot, for he stood with his fists on his hips, and yelled, "It was not either a lucky shot! My Pappy could shoot that hole a thousand times if'n he cared to."

Matt grinned at him, and turned to Jacob. "What do yeh say, Jacob, do yeh care to?" He held up his own medallion. "I got another medallion."

Jacob didn't answer, but set Hannah's stock upon the ground to reload.

Lil Jake cheered, followed by the crowd. He took his uncle's medallion, and propped it upon the slab. He began to return to his place in the crowd, but his uncle called him back and told him to sit in his Pappy's seat. The boy sat proud and tall.

Jacob took his time with the reloading. Half of shooting was careful loading he knew, but he was also in no hurry. He wanted to let the boy bask; he deserved it.

He looked at the target. *Matt's right, this is child's play.* He wanted a challenge; it'd been too long since he'd had one. He turned, and strode another twenty yards. He looked again at the medallion shining in the sun. Still too close. He went another ten yards. That was about right he reckoned. It'd be a challenge now; even for him.

He licked his finger, wet the sight, and settled Hannah to his shoulder. *God in Heaven, this sure feels good.* He squeezed the trigger.

The medallion did not move. For a moment he thought he had missed, but Lil Jake whooped, and ran to snatch it from the post crying, "Another dead center." He ran to his pappy, and showed it to him. Jacob saw it was indeed a dead center shot. He handed Hannah to the boy, and took the medallion. He gazed at it with pride for a moment, and then hung it about his grandson's neck.

"Its yers," he said, taking back his rifle. "Somethin' ta remember yer Pappy by when he's gone." The boy grinned up at him mutely. His shining eyes were the finest accolade Jacob had ever received. "Go on with yeh," he said, and gave the boy a shove. "Show it ta yer Ma."

The boy ran, and Jacob glanced at his brother. He was suddenly weary of the crowd; he wanted to leave. "Yeh comin'?"

Matt came, and the noise of the crowd soon abated. Jacob was glad.

He lifted the old rifle from his shoulder, and caressed its barrel. "Still a durn fine weapon, aint she?"

Matt slapped him on the back. "Still a durn fine man who bears her."